A Backstitch
Murder

A Quilter's Club Mystery

ABSOLUTELY AMAZING eBOOKS

Habent Sua Fata Libelli

ABSOLUTELY AMA⚡ING eBOOKS

Manhanset House
Shelter Island Hts., New York 11965-0342

bricktower@aol.com • tech@absolutelyamazingebooks.com
• absolutelyamazingebooks.com

Mentor Books is a joint imprint of
Absolutely Amazing eBooks
and AdLab Media Communications, LLC.

The Absolutely Amazing eBooks colophon is a trademark of
J. T. Colby & Company, Inc.

Library of Congress Cataloging-in-Publication Data
Rockwell, Marjory Sorrell.
A Backstitch Murder, A Quilter's Club Mystery #18.
p. cm.

1. FICTION / Mystery & Detective / Amateur Sleuth.
2. FICTION / Mystery & Detective / General.
3. FICTION / Thrillers / Suspense.
Fiction, I. Title.
ISBN: 978-1-955036-41-2, Trade Paper

November 2022

A Backstitch
Murder

A Quilter's Club Mystery

(Book 18)

Marjory Sorrell
Rockwell

A **Backstitch** is the strongest stitch that you can sew by hand. It is also one of the easier stitches to learn.

The Crustal Palace, Marengo
Cave, a US National Landmark.

Quilter's Club Mysteries

By Marjory Sorrell Rockwell

The Quilter's Club Quartet (Anthology 1)
The Quilter's Club Trio (Anthology 2)
The Quilter's Club Triple Stack (Anthology 3)
The Quilter's Club Threefold (Anthology 4)

The Underhanded Stitch (Book 1)
The Patchwork Puzzler (Book 2)
Coming Unraveled (Book 3)
Hemmed In (Book 4)
Sewed Up Tight (Book 5)
All Tangled Up (Book 6)
A Christmas Quit (Prequel – Book 7)
Needled (Book 8)
Stitch In Time (Book 9)
Cross Stitch (Book 10)
Fat Quarters (Book 11)
Stitch in the Ditch (Book 12)

Quilt Block (Book 13)
A Thimbleful of Murder (Book 14)
Sew Be It (Book 15)
Stab Stitching and Other Dangers (Book 16)
A Golden Needle and a Silver Bullet (Book 17)
A Backstitch Murder (Book 18)

**Available from
AbsolutelyAmazingEbooks.com**

Table of Contents

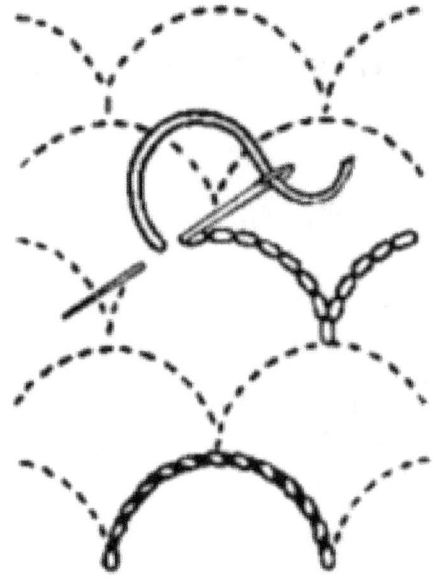

A **Backstitch** and its variants (*stem stitch, outline stitch,* and *split stitch*) are sewing stitches made backward in the general direction of the sewing. These small back-and-forth stitches form lines that are used to outline shapes and add fine detail to an embroidered picture. A strong utility stitch, it permanently attaches two pieces of fabric together.

Map of Marengo Cave

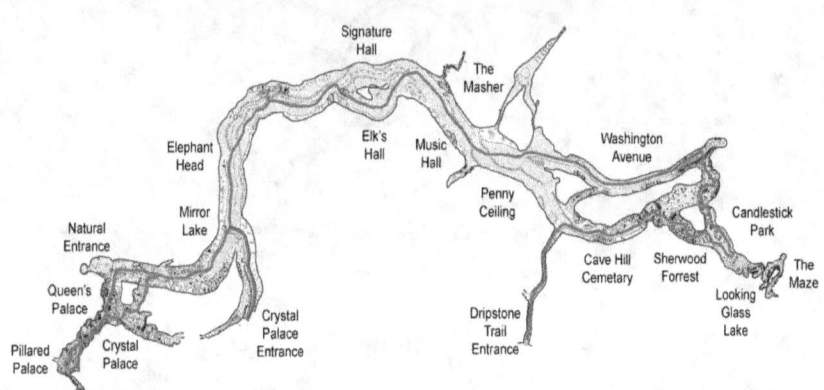

Chapter One

Crystal Power

Maddy Madison's daughter had never been the hippie type. Tilly had married her straight-laced husband Mark Tidemore while in college. She'd never worn beads in her hair or dressed in baggy tie-dyed T-shirts or burned her bra. Her musical tastes ran more to Karen Carpenter or Simon and Garfunkel than Dylan or Leonard Cohen. Woodstock took place before she was born. It was only recently that she got involved in New Agey things like Crystal Power.

Tilly's husband – once known in legal circles as Mark the Shark – was now the mayor of Caruthers Corners, a tiny town (pop. 2,812) tucked away in a bend of the Wabash River in a northeast corner of Indiana. The only crystal power he was familiar with was in the quartz mechanism of his $4,800 Grand Seiko SBGV238 wristwatch. He was worried about his wife's tenuous grasp with reality, a growing mindset that included fairies, ghosts, dragons ... and now magical crystals.

Any cultural historian can tell you that New Agers believe that crystals have holistic healing powers. Or bring luck. Or ward off evil spirits.

Others see it differently.

A crystallographer – a member of that branch of science concerned with the structure and properties of crystals – would explain that a crystal is a homogeneous solid substance having a natural geometrically regular form with symmetrically arranged plane faces, such as a clear transparent mineral like quartz or amethyst.

Maddy's husband Beau was likely to ramble on about crystal radios. He used to make them as a boy, sometimes able to pick up Wolfman Jack from Ciudad Acuña in Mexico or Alan Freed over in Cleveland. Those were the days. Rock and roll forever!

As for Police Chief Jim Purdue, he would lecture you on the dangers of crystal meth, a form of the drug methamphetamine, known for its ability to stimulate a user's central nervous system while becoming highly addictive. Illegal meth labs were an increasing concern in this part of the state.

Maddy's 16-year-old grandson N'yen might discuss "the crystalline sphere," which in ancient astronomy was postulated to be a transparent sphere of the heavens lying between the fixed stars and the *primum mobile*. This theory accounted for the precession of the equinox and other motions. But then again, the boy was studying astrophysics in an early enrollment program at Northwestern.

Maddy's granddaughter Aggie (Tilly's oldest) might refer to crystallization as a stage of gaining clarity in her writing. She was completing her first year at Yale, looking toward earning a law degree like her dad.

Maddy and her cronies at the Quilters Club sometimes stitched a Double Diamond Quilt, a crystal-like design that's very popular with advanced needlecrafters. The Quilters Club met on Tuesdays at the local Quilting Heritage Museum.

But Tilly saw crystals as being therapeutic. She had started collecting shiny rocks – opals, quartz, agates, geodes and the like. She had cemented an array of them across the dashboard of her new car, creating sort of a good luck shrine.

Mark was horrified to see the fine leather interior of a $50,800 Lexus ES 350 desecrated by "a pile of gravel," as he put it.

Fascinated by crystals, Tilly had planned a family outing to Marengo Cave, a US National Natural Landmark in Southern Indiana. She wanted to visit the wing known as the Crystal Palace.

That's where she would discover the dead body of Professor Jonathan Livingston Segal, the world-renown expert on troglofauna (animals that live in caves).

Who killed the prof?

Tilly swore a Morlock did it.

Chapter Two

Meet the Quilters Club

Madelyn "Maddy" Madison loved making quilts. But she valued the camaraderie of her quilter friends even more. They were more like sisters than members of a tiny quilting circle.

Elizabeth "Lizzie" Ridenour was the one most adept at quiltmaking. A three-time state champion, she managed the Hoople Quilting Heritage Museum. Her husband Edgar was a retired bank president.

Katherine "Cookie" Bentley headed up the Caruthers Corners Historical Society. It helped that she had an eidetic memory, a mental quirk that allowed her to recall facts and dates like a human encyclopedia. Her husband Ben was the largest landholder in the county.

Barbara Jo "Bootsie" Purdue's passion was rescuing animals, and she ran the Strays & Rescues Animal Shelter on the edge of town. Her hubby Jim was the local police chief.

Maddy Madison was the "grand dame" of the group, being married to Beauregard Hollingsworth Madison IV, a descendant of one of the Town Founders. That was worth a few bonus points on the town's social scale.

Back in 1829, three hardy pioneers – Col. Beauregard Hollingsworth Madison, Ferdinand Aloysius Jinks, and Jacob

Abernathy Caruthers – were leading a wagon train west when one of the Conestoga wagons broke down here on the banks of the Wabash, halting their westward trek and establishing the little town of Caruthers Corners in the new state of Indiana.

In addition to the four members of the Quilters Club, two of Maddy's grandchildren – Aggie (Tilly's daughter) and N'yen (Bill's adopted son) – had been accepted as junior members. But, truth be told, they were in it more for the sleuthing than the needlework.

The Quilters Club had gained a local reputation for solving crimes. Aside from their skills in stitching an array of magnificent quilts – Log Cabin Quilts, Crazy Quilts, Charm Quilts, even Fancy Feathers Appliqué Quilts – the gals had unraveled several puzzling mysteries that involved everything from patchwork quilts stuffed with rare "watermelon dollars" to Viking treasures, Lost Boys who turned up 30 years later, Ferdinand Jinks' buried gold, the Beasley ghost, UFOs, magic acts that bring back the dead, a mad scientist who tried to poison the town's water supply, thieves who stole an antediluvian fossil collection, and phony historic quilts that needed exposing.

For Aggie and N'yen, it was like playing a real-life game of Clue. But now they were off at college, leaving only their young friend Cecilia Jackson in their stead. Sissy was showing talent as a quilter ... and as an amateur detective.

~ ~ ~

The Quilters Club had just completed a large community project, sewing a huge wall quilt that would cover one whole side of the meeting room that took up most of the first floor in the Town Hall.

A Pictorial Quilt, it replicated a popular postcard showing the town in all its colorful splendor. Including a **WELCOME TO CARUTHERS CORNERS** banner scrolling across the top of the quilt.

A photo of it made the front page of the *Burpyville Gazette*. Below the fold, but on the front page nonetheless.

Now, the four gals were turning their attention to making Crazy Quilts, patchworks with no two pieces alike. It was a good way to use up all those stray scraps of fabric piling up in the Quilting Heritage Museum's craft room.

Crazy Quilts have an interesting history. Inspired by the asymmetrical art in the 1876 Philadelphia Exposition, the making of crazy quilts became quite the rage. To Victorians, the word "crazy" meant broken or crazed into splinters – a good description for the various triangles and other odd shapes that gave these quilts their name.

From a distance, Crazy Quilts look like confetti sewn together to make eye-dazzling coverlets. Although their design may appear to be haphazard, Crazy Quilts are carefully planned. An 1883 article in *The Chester Times* (Chester, PA) explained how they were made:

> "If your pieces are of good size, and all fresh and handsome, one way is to cut out blocks of cotton cloth, either square or diamond-shape. Cut enough blocks to make the quilt the desired size, then paste on the pieces of silk, satin, or velvet; lap the edges and turn the upper one under; then cover every seam with feather-stitch, cross-stitch, or any fancy stitch you can invent."

According to *American Quilting History*, "Making a Crazy Quilt was also popular for fundraising. Sometimes churchwomen would write to famous people asking for a piece of clothing that could be incorporated into the quilt they were making to raise money to help the missionaries, build a new church or other worthy cause. What a great conversation piece such a quilt would be!"

Maddy and her friends were very pleased with their progress. In a few weeks they would hold a Quilt Sale to raise money for the Museum. Despite its occasional funding by Maddy's personal trust, it could always use a new roof, furnace repairs, or a fresh coat of paint. In a single word, upkeep!

Maddy Madison had not been born a Trust Fund Baby. She had inherited the money recently, when it was discovered she'd been a secret love child of Herbert Hoople, one of the world-famous Hoople Quadruplets. The Quads used to be the town's greatest claim to fame ... before it was revealed that they were a fraud. Four unrelated children passed off as a biological miracle. But by the time the charade was uncovered, the Hooples had become the wealthiest family in Caruthers Corners.

Lucky Maddy, it was like hitting BINGO in the Game of Life.

She and her family had been invited to live in Hoople Mansion, the big castle on a hillock overlooking the town of Caruthers Corners. It was a bit ostentatious for her tastes, but this was the "family" manse.

Chapter Three

A New New Ager

To everyone's surprise, Tilly Tidemore had recently embraced the New Age Movement. This broad spectrum of alternate spiritual beliefs became popular during the '70s, but Maddy's daughter had just discovered this fusion of Mind, Body, and Spirit.

New Age draws heavily on the work of Emanuel Swedenborg and Franz Mesmer, as well as such influences as UFO religions of the 1950s and the counterculture of the 1960s.

Crystal Power is a large part of this postmodern belief system. New Agers are convinced crystals have the ability to boost low energy, prevent bad energy, release blocked energy, or simply bring luck.

The word *crystal* is derived from the Ancient Greek word κρύσταλλος, meaning both "ice" and "rock crystal." Common examples of crystals include diamonds, snowflakes, and even common table salt.

Mainstream thinking considers Crystal Therapy to be a pseudoscience, its healing powers more placebo than medicinal. But it has many followers. Not just old hippies and New Agers, but also Wiccans and good witches who use stones in their spellwork.

Nonetheless, crystal healing is mentioned in Plato's account of Atlantis (Atlanteans supposedly used crystals to read minds and transmit thoughts) and in the records of Ancient Sumerians (they used them in magical formulas).

Crystal healing can be traced back to such early cultures as Egypt, Mesopotamia, India, Greece, and Rome. Buddhists have used crystals as prayer beads for meditation for centuries.

Crystals are considered to be gemstones. They often are used in jewelry. Like the ads say, diamonds are forever.

Tilly Tidemore had a large collection of bracelets and bangles, all neatly displayed in a large glass cabinet. Everything from an expensive diamond tennis bracelet to cheap agate wristlets. This gemstone jewelry had been a bridge to her embracing Crystal Power.

Some of these bangles were made with stones said to emanate magic qualities. Or at least that's what they told her at Rock-et Power, a new rock shop in Burpyville, the next town over. She had become a regular customer.

~ ~ ~

Rock-et Power was managed by Margie Yost's cousin, Cynthia. Margie was the purple-haired (this week) proprietor of Helen of Troy Spa and Beauty Saloon, where Maddy and the girls got their hair done. Lizzie had a weekly appointment, careful to remove any traces of gray from her flaming red locks.

Cynthia Yost (Cindy to her friends, which included everybody) was a scatterbrained flower child. Her parents had been part of a '60s commune. Her birthname had been Feather. People said the 50-ish woman had been conceived at Woodstock. Margie refused to discuss this side of the family, claiming Cindy's Mom and Dad were in a Witness Protection Program. Something about the Weather Underground.

Cindy never mentioned them either. She was too busy extolling the inner powers within crystals. The little shop was thriving.

Tilly was becoming quite the acolyte. Crystal Power was almost like a religion. She'd become obsessed with the magical properties within rocks and such.

~ ~ ~

Tilly's family trip to the Crystal Palace had been planned well in advance. Reservations were made and paid for online; the route carefully planned out by AAA. In addition to TripTiks, Triple-A provided a useful phone app that included online maps.

Although all of them had been born and raised in the Hoosier State, not a single member of the family had ever been to Marengo Cave – even though it is billed as "Indiana's Most Visited Natural Attraction." It's always like that, isn't it? Most people in New York City never visit the Empire State Building unless they're entertaining visitors from out of town.

Maddy was about to break that pattern, having promised that she and Beau would visit Marengo Cave with Tilly and her husband Mark on this coming Wednesday.

Little did she expect to encounter a dead body there.

As you may have read in that article in the *Burpyville Gazette* by crime reporter Penelope Heath, it was Tilly Tidemore who discovered the bludgeoned professor. Tilly also claimed she saw the murderer. That's where the story got a little vague. Nobody at the paper wanted to say the wife of a local mayor had identified the killer as a subterranean monster straight out of an 1895 science-fiction novel. That was crazy, right?

Chapter Four

Inside the Cave

Marengo Cave was discovered in 1883 by two children who were exploring a sinkhole in Crawford County, an out-of-the-way spot at the southern edge of the state. Designated a US National Natural Landmark in 1984, Marengo is one of four "show caves" in Indiana.

At first, Blanche Heistand and her younger brother Orris thought they had found diamonds because of the sparkling flowstone formations that their candles reflected on inside the cave. When local folks heard of this discovery, they came en masse to see the array of stalactites hanging from the limestone ceilings. Some began breaking off souvenirs, but the landowner quickly put a stop to that, thus preserving it as it one of the more pristine caves in the US.

And within two days he was charging an admission fee for sightseers.

Still privately owned, Marengo Cave remains a commercial enterprise. Open all year long, it offers two different walking tours – (1) the Crystal Palace and (2) the Dripstone. The Crystal Palace Tour covers one-third mile of the cave. The Dripstone Trail offers over one mile of subterranean passages to explore.

One of the longest caves in the state, Marengo stretches all told almost 5 miles underneath its mountainside.

Southern Indiana is home to over 4,000 known caves. Only a short distance from Marengo Cave is Indiana Caverns (the longest cave), Bluespring Caverns (with its subterranean river voyage), and Squire Boone Caverns (where Daniel Boone's brother hid from Indians) – promoted together as the Indiana Cave Trail. If you visit all four, you get a free T-shirt.

~ ~ ~

Tilly Tidemore and her family arrived in the tiny town of Marengo (pop. 828) just before noon that Wednesday. Mark was driving; her Mom and Dad comfortably seated in the backseat. She had insisted they take her 2020 powder-blue Lexus. She said the crystal shrine on the dashboard would resonate with the Crystal Palace wing of Marengo Cave. Mark just rolled his eyes; Maddy and Beau offered no comment.

Tilly's therapist didn't seem to be making much progress. She had now adopted an invisible friend called Herbert. He was a Morlock, she said, just like in H.G. Wells' *The Time Machine*. She said he was the one who wanted to visit the cave, that he was homesick. Morlocks, as every sci-fi reader knows, live underground.

Marengo Cave turned out to be a three-hour drive from Caruthers Corners. The AAA directions had been easy to follow: Go south on Indiana S.R. 37 to English, then east on Indiana S.R. 64 for 8 miles. The town is located in the Blue River Basin of Southern Indiana, a karst region that claims over 1,000 nearby caves.

These karstlands are characterized by underlying St. Genevieve limestone. Acidic water gradually dissolved these rocks, leaving behind sinkholes, seeps, and caves. According to current geologic theory, Marengo Cave began to form approximately one million years ago.

When the cave first opened to the public back in 1883, admission was only 25¢. Now it costs $28.95 for both tours, the Crystal Palace and the Dripstone Trail. However, opting just for the Crystal Palace Tour knocked ten bucks off the ticket price per person.

The two tours have separate entrances, the Crystal Palace opening just to the left of the gift shop, the Dripstone far off to the right. After descending to the second level, the Crystal Palace Tour is an easy, well-lit stroll on a paved underground pathway. It takes about 40 minutes, winding through formation-filled rooms and past huge flowstone deposits.

The Madisons and the Tidemores came well prepared. The Marengo Cave website had furnished a helpful list of what to wear:

- Two layers of old warm clothes. Arms and legs must be covered. (You may never want to wear them again due to the mud and dirt, it says.)
- Boots or other old sturdy shoes, high top or lace up. (No Crocs or water shoes.)
- Kneepads (Highly Recommended).
- Gloves (Highly Recommended).

It also suggested that one should bring along:
- A complete change of clothes (to wear home).
- Another pair of shoes (to wear home).
- Shower accessories such as towel, soap, etc. (Trust us, you will want to wash off, it advices.)
- Plastic bag (for the muddy clothes).

No need to bring any gear. A Petzl helmet with a mounted LED light is supplied. And you get to keep the light afterward.

Maddy was glad she brought her Lands' End puffer jacket. The temperature inside the cave remains a constant 52° year round. Not exactly cold, but the older she got the chillier she got. Brrrr.

For the Crystal Palace Tour, there are three sections – the Pillared Palace, the Queen's Palace, and the eponymous Crystal Palace itself. Although Marengo's two walking tours have separate entrances, they actually link up at the far end of the Dripstone Trail. For that reason, the Dripstone's exit is the same opening as the Crystal Palace's entrance.

The cave provides a winding underground maze with places that bear names like Candlestick Park, Sherwood Forest, Washington Avenue, Elephant Head, Signature Hall, Masher, Looking Glass Lake, the Pig Pen. There's the Music Hall where a local band used to played concerts; a Pulpit where religious services were held; Elk Hall where fraternal groups sometimes met; a dance hall; a stage for Shakespearean plays; and the famous Penny Ceiling where people toss coins that stick to the gummy roof of the cavern ("like a reverse wishing well").

During the 1962 Cuban Missile Crisis, the cave was designated as a Civil Defense shelter, although it was never used. Later on, overnight youth camps slept here; people got married in the cave; and in the winter there's even a night of underground caroling. Locals also used it as a refuge when a deadly tornado blew through town in 2004.

Marengo is considered "a very safe cave."

~ ~ ~

The Crystal Palace Tour begins through a man-made entrance constructed in 1910. The small metal door signals this is not a journey for the claustrophobic.

The original entrance has been closed off. It was thought to be too dangerous, with its 156 damp, slippery steps leading into the depth of the cave.

Maddy and her family joined the small tour group – about a dozen tourists in all today. The guide was a young carrot-topped man who introduced himself as Lenny Ray Scroggins. He gave them a rundown of what to expect:

"Mud, lots of mud.

"Slippery footing in places.

"Low passages where you have to duck your head.

"And absolute darkness, except for the headlamps, your flashlight, and the faint lighting which runs along the passageways," Lenny Ray ticked off the list.

On the Dripstone tour the lights are turned off for a moment to let visitors experience the pitch-blackness of a cave's interior. But you don't get that on the Crystal Palace tour. It's sort of like the Bunny Slope at a ski resort – an easy-does-it run for first-timers. Or in Beau and Maddy's case, old-timers. After all, they were both in their 60s now.

Lenny Ray explained what kind of speleothems they would find inside the cave. Speleothem is Greek for "cave deposit," or cave formations.

- A **stalactite** is an icicle-like formation of calcium carbonate created over time by water dripping from the ceiling of a cave.
- Sometimes the dripping also creates a finger of calcium carbonate rising from the floor, a formation known as a **stalagmite**. Note: A way to differentiate

between the two is that stalactite has a "c" in it for *ceiling*, and stalagmite has a "g" in it for *ground*.

- When the two formations touch (after centuries of dripping), they form a **column**.
- **Helictites** are formations that change their axis from the vertical during their growth cycle, branching out into curving or spiral shapes. The helictite begins as a **soda-straw**-like tube formed by individual drops of water depositing calcium carbonate around the rim of a speleothem.
- **Flowstone** formations are common on the Crystal Palace side of the cave. Flowstone occurs when water rich in calcium carbonate flows along the walls or floor of a cave, depositing layers of calcite. These broad sheets can be as smooth as a lava flow, as glossy as glass, or look like hanging curtains and draperies.
- **Cave popcorn** (also called **cave coral**) are the small, knobby rock clusters that resemble popped corn.
- **Rimstone dams** are formed as water flows over the rim of a rock shelf, "like water overflowing a sink." This results in calcite deposits around the edge of the dam.

"Remember these formations," joked Lenny Ray. "There may be a pop quiz later." Cave guide humor, no doubt.

~ ~ ~

Entering the cave, the group scrambled down a steep ramp alongside a rushing stream of water. The rivulet cascaded past them, making a splashy 10-foot drop into Mirror Lake on the level below.

Marengo Cave has three layers. Reaching the lake, they found themselves standing on the muddy floor of the second (middle) level.

Mirror Lake is only 3 to 6 inches deep, but the water mirrors the rock formations above it, creating the illusion of depth. You could easily mistake it as a view into a lower cavern. Maddy and her family found the sight breathtaking. Everybody *ooo*'d and *ahhh*'d.

Although the pathway is paved, there are no railings. It can be wet and slippery in places. The caverns are actually well lighted, showing off the formations and making tourists surer of their footing. The two walking tours are comfortable strolls, unlike the special Adventure Tours into side passages that involve crawling through narrow, muddy crevices like the Pig Pen.

Following the narrow path around the lake, they came upon the first major stalagmite, a formation known as Mount Vesuvius. Standing nearly five feet tall, this upside-down cone resembles an erupting volcano with a plume of "smoke" rising from its peak. Maddy got a nice snapshot of it with her Nikon Coolpix P1000. The camera's 125x optical zoom brought the subject up close, as if she could reach out and touch it.

However, in a "show" cave, no touching is allowed. Even very small formations take thousands of years to develop. And the oils from your hands can compromise the growth of stalactites and stalagmites.

Nearby, they spotted a flat structure, about 4 feet by 6 feet, that resembles an aircraft carrier.

Farther on was a limestone shelf called the Tom-Tom, where Lenny Ray produced a rubber mallet and beat out a halting tune on it. *Bong! Bing! Bong!*

A craggy series of flowstones resembled peaks of a mountain range. Naturally, they are nicknamed The Rocky Mountains.

Continuing through the caverns, they came to Discovery Falls, a marvelous stream of water that cascades through a large gap in the ceiling. The waterfall conceals the original entrance to Marengo Cave. There, a multimedia show is projected onto the stone wall, recreating that historic moment in 1883 when Blanche and Orris Hiestand discovered the cave.

A few steps away, a series of moist stalagmites in different shades of brown, red, and black rise from the floor like a bed of nails, their color differences due to the varying mineral content of the rocks. White streaks indicate a high calcite content while the black is due to manganese. Layers of red are the result of a dense clay content. Some of the formations have swirls of all three colors, like a parfait.

Squeezing through a tight corridor of stalactite columns, the group found themselves surrounded by "cave bacon," a term used to describe draping, layered stalactites.

At the halfway point of the tour, they came to Queens Palace, an area named for the large chandelier-shaped rocks that hang from the ceiling. If you catch them at the right angle with a flashlight the structures sparkle due to the high mineral deposits in the rock.

After passing through Pillared Palace's floor-to-ceiling columns, they reached the cavern that the tour is named after, The Crystal Palace. People say that each corner resembles a different room within a vast palace. The Crystal Palace is famous for its sparkling ceiling. The millions of deposited minerals in the ceiling glitter in the light like a large disco ball above a dance floor.

Maddy got a good picture of The Rock of Ages, with its enormous flowing formations, covered in black, white, and brown stripes. Standing about 40 feet high, the pillars resemble a giant melting wedding cake.

And finally the Pipe Organ, there in the spectacular space where visitors are treated to a light and sound show – with piped in music and flashing colored lights.

~ ~ ~

Lenny Ray pointed out that they were now standing 150 feet below the old cemetery that's adjacent to the gift shop. It was a little unnerving to realize they were beneath dozens of graves, with bodies moldering in their coffins just above their heads.

From here, they began the circular hike back towards Mirror Lake and the adjacent exit. The tour had covered about 1/3rd mile, and lasted just under an hour.

Tilly was disappointed that the Crystal Palace didn't have any actual crystals. The ceiling sparkled with flecks of minerals, but she had been hoping for big prisms of quartz or chunks of azurite. Even garnets or malachite or fool's gold.

She told herself that she would've had better luck at the gemstone mining attraction located just outside the cave. There, kids pan for treasure, keeping any pretty rocks they find in the sluice. She might have found a small ruby or emerald – a real crystal!

Despite her invisible friend's recommendation, Tilly knew she'd picked the wrong cave. She would have been much happier visiting, say, Crystal Cave at Sequoia National Park in California.

Or maybe Crater of Diamonds State Park in Arkansas – a 911-acre park that is the only diamond-digging site in America where the public can search for diamonds in the fields and can keep them.

Or better still, the Cave of Crystals, a natural wonder where selenite crystals glimmer in dark recesses beneath the Naica Mine in Chihuahua, Mexico. However, that cave is extremely hot, its temperature a steady 136°F.

But with that cave being 2,563 miles away, Tilly would have to settle for souvenirs from Marengo Cave's rock shop.

Pouting, she lagged behind the tour group. Feeling a cold breeze, she turned in that direction and spotted a bronze plaque affixed to a boulder identifying this as the entrance to BLOWING BAT CRAWL.

The plaque explained:

ON JUNE 14, 1992, EXPERIENCED CAVE EXPLORERS DUG THROUGH THE FINAL TIGHT SPOT IN THE "BAT CRAWL" TO DISCOVER THE LARGEST CAVE PASSAGE EVER FOUND IN AN INDIANA CAVE.

Curious, Tilly pointed her flashlight toward this side passage. It was more like a narrow crevice in the rock. No wonder they called it a "crawl." She moved to the side for a better look, revealing the limestone floor behind the large boulder that held the metal plaque. The light reflected off something bright. A crystal perhaps?

She stepped closer.

No, it wasn't a piece of quartz or a chunk of amethyst. It was a reflection off the lens on a pair of steel-rimmed eyeglasses. Had someone lost their spectacles here in the cave?

She stepped closer to pick them up. She would turn them in at the gift shop in case anyone was looking for them. That's when she saw the body, likely the owner of said spectacles. He looked … dead.

Just beyond the body, at the edge of the illumination from the Crystal Palace's overhead lighting, she saw something move. It was something big and hulking, a humanoid shape with two glowing eyes. The murderer perhaps?

"Umph," the shape said, extending a gnarled hand in her direction.

Tilly screamed, her shrill voice sending an echo throughout the surrounding limestone passages like a banshee's howl. That's the last thing she recalled until her eyelids flickered open to reveal the people from the cave tour bending over her and her husband's voice saying, "Hon, are you all right?"

Chapter Five

An Unreliable Narrator

"**I**s your wife on any kind of medication?" the sheriff asked Mark Tidemore. "Y'know, something that might have altered her perception."

"Are you asking if my wife is a druggie?"

"Now, now, Mr. Tidemore. She said she's been under a therapist's care. I figure he's prescribing some sort of mood stabilizer or antipsychotic."

"She's not crazy."

"I didn't say that. It's just that those prescriptions – Xanax or Thorazine, stuff like that – can cause hallucinations or impair one's thinking."

"Are you suggesting my wife merely imagined that dead man? I saw him myself."

"Oh, the dead man's real alright. We just identified him, a college professor. Said to be an expert on creepy crawlies that live in caves. This guy – Dr. Jonathan Segal – was doing research on local bats, trying to determine if they might carry some kind of Wuhan virus like COVID. The caves hereabouts are home to over 100,000 Indiana Bats."

"What's your point, Sheriff?"

"Your wife said she saw the killer."

"That's right."

"She said Dr. Segal was murdered by a Morlock. That's a fictional creature from a science-fiction novel, I'm told."

"H.G. Wells."

"What? This Morlock had a name?"

"No, that's the author of the science-fiction novel. H.G. Wells created Morlocks in his book *The Time Machine*."

"Then you agree that Morlocks are not real."

"Of course."

"But your wife said one killed Dr. Segal."

Mark the Shark took a deep breath, then exhaled it slowly. "My wife has been having some fantasy issues. Sometimes her version of reality gets a little blurry. I doubt she imagined this killer. After all, we do have a dead man. But her perception of him may be a bit confused."

"Confused? She says the murderer is some kind of monster who dwells underground. I could never put her on the stand even if she was able to identify the murderer in a lineup."

"I understand. So let us sign our statements and we'll get out of your hair, head back up to Caruthers Corners. Sorry we couldn't be more help."

"I'm afraid it's not that simple."

"Oh? Why not?"

"Mr. Tidemore, I've checked you out. You used to be a high-powered lawyer. So you'll understand my position. Dr. Segal had just been bashed on the head with a rock. Your wife was the only one in that part of the cave, the tour group having moved on without her. There was no one else there to have killed him. That makes her a prime suspect."

"What about the man my wife saw?"

"A Morlock? Would you go into a court with that as your defense?"

"Not a Morlock, but SODDI – Some Other Dude Did It. That will have to be the defense if you arrest Tilly. If she didn't do it, somebody else did."

"Good luck with that."

At that point, Maddy spoke up. "Sheriff Barneswell, surely you don't believe my daughter committed this crime. The evidence suggests otherwise."

The lawman shifted his gaze, as if noticing the silver-haired lady for the first time. "The evidence?" he repeated.

"Yes," continued Maddy. Her voice calm and authoritative in tone. "I'm sure an experienced officer like yourself has noticed the discrepancies."

"What discrepancies?"

"Well, from what I could see back there at the cave, the professor had been struck on the top of his head. Likely the cause of death."

"That's right."

"But he was a tall, lanky man. Maybe six-feet-two, I'd say. A real beanstalk. And my daughter is barely five-four. She wasn't tall enough to strike the good professor on top of his head with a blunt instrument."

"A rock most likely."

"Whatever."

"Maybe he was sitting down."

"On that damp ground? The place was as wet as a mud puddle."

"Or maybe she was standing on one of them – whattaya call 'em? – stalagmites."

"Those Marengo Cave guides wouldn't let us touch any of those stalactites ... or stalagmites. Ecological protection and all that. Besides, if someone stood atop one, you'd find scuff marks from the shoes. I'm willing to bet there were none."

"None that we've seen yet. My crime scene guys are in there taking a closer look." That was a slight exaggeration. A small Sheriff's Department, he had no CSI team; only two young deputies.

Maddy continued, her voice sounding reasonable. "Assuming you can't find any marks, I'd think you'll have to let her go. She could not have physically committed the crime."

"Well –"

"She's got you there," smiled Mark Tidemore.

"Say, is she a lawyer too?" the Sheriff nodded toward Maddy.

"No, she's a quilter."

~ ~ ~

"Honest, it was a Morlock," insisted Tilly on the drive home. "He was holding a rock in his hand. The one he used to hit that guy on the head with."

"How do you know it was a Morlock?" pressed her mother. "What did he look like?"

"Big and muddy with glowing yellow eyes. Like Herbie." Tilly was huddled in her corner of the passenger's seat, her husband behind the wheel.

"Like who?"

"Herbie, my Morlock friend. Except Herbie's invisible. This one wasn't. He was standing there in front of that big crack in the rock – Bat Something, it was called according to a sign."

"Blowing Bat Crawl," Maddy supplied. She was leaning forward in the backseat of the Lexus, concerned about her daughter's well-being. Beau sat stiffly beside his wife, his usual taciturn self, taking it all in. Wasn't every day that the family encountered a murder. Well, not exactly.

Truth was, as a member of the Quilters Club, Maddy had seen her share of murders. Being amateur detectives, the gals had been drawn into more than a few mysterious deaths, but never one committed by a fictional creature like a Morlock. There had to be a rational explanation, she told herself.

Maddy couldn't wait to get back to Caruthers Corners and share the details with Lizzie, Cookie, and Bootsie. Maybe they would have a few ideas about this strange death in a subterranean chamber of Marengo Cave. And this imaginary, murderous Morlock.

"All the people on the tour were accounted for," Beau said out loud, as if talking with himself. "Twelve of us went in with the guide; twelve came out. No one else there."

"Might have been more people," mused Mark. "There's that second tour into the Dripstone side of the cave. The two passages connect. Matter of fact, the Dripstone folks go in their entrance, but exit through ours."

"But they would have had to pass us," Maddy pointed out. "And nobody did. Tilly was alone back there."

"Except for the murdered man and the Morlock," corrected Mark. Sticking with the SODDI theory.

"It wasn't Herbie," interjected Tilly. "He didn't do it."

"Who?"

"My Morlock. The one who wanted to go visit the cave."

"I thought that was your idea," said Beau.

"Not exactly. I wanted to go see the crystals. But Herbie was longing to spend some time in a subterranean lair. I think he's a bit homesick."

"Where *is* Herbie right now?" asked Tilly's husband.

"Right here in the front seat beside me. That's why I'm scooched in the corner. It's a tight fit."

Mark frowned. "Can we see him? Can he – what's the word? – materialize."

"Sorry, but he doesn't want to. Herbie's shy around humans. Except for me. He likes me, follows me around all the time. Like a dog. A 7-foot-tall dog."

Maddy asked the $64,000 question. "Did Herbie recognize the murderer? After all, they are fellow Morlocks."

That caught Tilly by surprise. "I don't know. He never said."

"Can you ask him?"

"Sure, Herbie was standing right beside me when I spotted the killer at that windy side passage. He got a good look at the killer too."

Chapter Six

Meanwhile Back at the
Quilting Museum

Lizzie was preparing for the exhibit of the Tristan and Isolde Quilt, a fragment of the oldest medieval quilt in the world. Recently, the Guicciardini family of San Francisco and Venice, Italy, had donated it to the Hoople Quilting Heritage Museum. A generous gesture.

As usual, Cookie and Bootsie were pitching in, helping Lizzie with the task of putting on a major exhibition, one that might even rate a squib in the Arts & Leisure section of *The New York Times*. The Tristan and Isolde Quilt was truly a big deal. Maddy would have been there to help too, except for the family outing to that cave down south. Maddy's daughter had insisted.

Not talking behind their friend's back – it would have been the same conversation if she'd been there – but they shared their concerns about Tilly's mental health. Not only was Tilly's mom their very best-est friend in the whole wide world, but Tilly's daughter Aggie was an honorary member of the Quilters Club.

Aggie – off at Yale – was old enough to take care of herself, but what about her younger sisters, the ones she jokingly called "The Terrible Trio"? And Mark Tidemore was mayor of Caruthers Corners. What would the town do if he got distracted by his wife's "condition"?

That new therapist didn't seem to be making much headway. Located over in Burpyville, Tilly saw him twice a week. Dr. Eichmann Fogle said it was a schizophreniform disorder, an ongoing malady that can manifest such symptoms as delusions, hallucinations, and social withdrawal.

At first, Tilly's pretense at being a fairy princess seemed cute, a playful eccentricity. Then came a fascination with unicorns and dragons and other cryptozoological fictions. And more recently spiritualism, those seances conducted by a crystal-gazing fraud known as Madame Flora. Now Tilly was enamored with crystal therapy and invisible friends.

A shame, in that Tilly's mother and daughter were themselves rock-steady intellects firmly grounded in reality – not alternate facts.

Maybe it was that Crackleton bloodline ...?

A few years back, Maddy Madison had learned that she had been adopted. No big deal, especially when her biological father turned out to be one of the world-famous and immensely wealthy Hoople Quadruplets.

That's how Maddy and Tilly and their families came to live in the Hoople Mansion, that gigantic monolith overlooking the town. Perched next to it on a twin hillock was the Perricock Museum of Science and History where Cookie worked.

All that was fine and good, a windfall of riches. But then it came out that the Hoople Quads had been a big fraud, not really a polyzygotic miracle of birth, but adopted children deliberately passed off as quadruplets. They had even appeared on the cover of *Time* Magazine. Quite *à cause du scandale* as the French would say.

And with this came the revelation that Maddy's father had been one of the unwanted offspring of Granny Crackleton, the crazy witch woman who headed that consanguineous clan up at Crackleton Crossing. Her inbred progeny included a carnival freak-show of damaged individuals, descendants displaying such medical disorders as microcephaly, polydactylism, dwarfism, hypertrichosis, and even the rare "vanishing twin" syndrome.

Granny herself was said to be Mad as a Hatter. Schizophrenia, some said.

Technically, Granny Crackleton was Maddy's grandmother. That made her Tilly's great-grandmother. Had those schizo genes skipped a few generations.

However, that was a question nobody wanted to say aloud.

~ ~ ~

"Did you hear about Harry Teague?" Bootsie Purdue changed the subject. Harry was one of her husband's deputies, so she had the inside scoop. "He married Penelope Heath last weekend. It was a civil service with a justice of the peace over in Burpyville."

"Do tell," said Lizzie. A magnet for gossip. "Isn't Penny Heath that reporter at the *Burpyville Gazette*?"

"The very same," Bootsie nodded vigorously, causing her excess poundage to jiggle. Her diet wasn't working. Thank goodness Police Chief Jim Purdue had a thing for Ruebenesque women. "Harry and Penny used to be an item," she continued. "Then they took a break. I guess this says the break's over."

"A cop and an I'm-gonna-bust-this-town-wide-open newspaper reporter – what could go wrong with that?"

chuckled Cookie Bentley. She pushed her glasses back onto the bridge of her nose, straightening them in the process. With her forget-me-not memory, she could recall Penny Heath's first bylined story in the *Gazette*, an ambitious piece headlined **B'VILLE MAYOR HEADS CRIME RING.**

Turned out, Burpyville's then-mayor Sean McGonagall had been working with the FBI on a public-official bribery case, a sting operation, making him a hero and Penny a cub reporter facing suspension. But Penelope Heath had clawed her way back into the publisher's good graces with a scoop on Salvatore Milano – A/K/A "Sal the Whisperer" – being elevated to Indy's top crime boss. Sal's rival had met an untimely demise when he fell into a cement mixer.

Harry Teague had been her unnamed source. He maintained a good network of reliable snitches. That had saved Penny's bacon, f'sure.

"Should we throw them a delayed reception," posited Lizzie Ridenour. She was a social butterfly at heart. Her flamingo-red hair (Lady Clairol's Sweet Cherry Dark Red) signaled an exuberant nature.

"Not a bad idea," agreed Bootsie. "After all, Harry is my husband's chosen successor as police chief."

"Is Jim planning to resign ... again?" asked Cookie. She liked to keep up with the latest news. "History in the making," she called it.

"Soon. And I think it will stick this time around," declared Bootsie. She would be glad to have her husband home full-time to help her watch after the dogs. Aside from the dozens of canines she cared for at the Strays & Rescues shelter, Bootsie had adopted six or eight on her own. Sometimes she lost count.

In retaliation, Jim had adopted a retired K-9 German Shepherd for himself. Once a trained crime-scene cadaver dog with the Chicago Police Department, the big pooch had turned into an oversized lapdog. Although supposedly Jim's pet, he followed Bootsie around like a puppy behind its mommy.

"Jim's retirement likely would've taken last time around," commented Cookie, "if his successor hadn't got himself killed."

"Yes, poor Evers Gochnauer," sighed Lizzie. "Let's hope Harry Teague doesn't face the same fate." Evers had been killed on the job.

"Being police chief is very dangerous," averred Bootsie. Aggrandizing her chubby hubby. But everyone knew Chief Jim Purdue's greatest threat was the jelly donuts at Cozy Café. He and his deputies spent most of their time handing out parking tickets and helping old ladies cross the street. Caruthers Corners had a low crime rate, despite the occasional murder cases the Quilters Club took on.

Evers had been a rare exception. Indiana has seen only 19 officers killed in the line of duty since 2010.

Maddy's granddaughter Aggie liked to call the Quilters Club a "quasi-detective agency." But the original foursome considered themselves nothing more than a quilting bee that sometimes got involved in solving mysteries – a civic duty.

~ ~ ~

Harry Teague still owned his family homestead on the upper end of the county, but he and his new wife had put a down payment on a starter home in Wabash Acres, the development halfway between Caruthers Corners and Burpyville on Highway 21.

Wabash Acres was more of a retirement village, but the prices were right for a couple just starting out. And its location was perfect, with Harry working for the Caruthers Corners

Police Department and Penny still on the staff of the *Burpyville Gazette*, one town over. It wasn't a bad commute for either of them. And the traffic on the Burpyville Highway was never very heavy, except during the annual Watermelon Days festival.

Penny Heath (she was still using that byline despite her marriage) had just scored another front page story, securing her new position as the paper's crime reporter. The above-the-fold piece was a follow-up on the recent Henny Penny Murder, as the *Gazette* had tagged it, the falling death of Dr. Henry Pendergast, the late director of the Perricock Museum of Science and History. She revealed that the "murderer" had been none other than the former librarian of Caruthers Corners, Mary Alice Hegler. But the police had called it an "accidental homicide." And the death certificate signed by Dr. Franklin Delano Medford confirmed this contradictory finding.

Mary Alice and her brother, a stage magician known as The Great Wizardini, had disappeared – literally – in a flash of blue smoke following the death of Henny Penny. However, with Mary Alice being a beloved town figure, nobody had gone looking for them. No charges had been filed. The fall had been ruled accidental. Her disappearance unnecessary.

Penny Health had her new hubby to thank for this insider's information. Some people think Chief Purdue put him up to spilling the story. Leaking it out there to protect Mary Alice Hegler's reputation from rumors and innuendo.

The citizens of Caruthers Corners had responded favorably to the story of accidental death, the Heglers' exit lamented by all. A back corner of the town's new library featured the Great Wizardini Magic Room, a place for mothers to park their children while browsing the bookshelves. And a Mary Alice Hegler Coffee Bar occupied another corner, providing a gathering spot for local housewives who were looking for a morning break.

The Heglers' adopted niece – Dorothy Stargazer – succeeded Mary Alice as town librarian. She had organized the new library (the old library had been blown away by that terrible 2018 tornado) in a wing of the Perricock Museum.

In another section of the museum, a room has been dedicated to the late director. The Henry Pendergast Gallery houses a nearly complete brontosaurus skeleton, a find that Henny Penny made in South Dakota back in the late '90s.

The museum's new director – Dr. William Worth Wellington – had raised the funds to have the sauropod fossils put together by a team from the American Museum of Natural History. Assembling a dinosaur skeleton was tricky, like solving a gigantic 3-D puzzle. Both time-consuming and costly, and requiring a great deal of expertise. Wild Willie (as Dr. Wellington was known in paleontological circles) is considered one of the foremost experts on Diplodocids, the family of dinosaurs that includes brontosaurs and apatosaurs. He had studied at Penn State under the late Dr. Pendergast, a point in his favor when being considered for the museum job.

~ ~ ~

Penelope Heath was doing a follow-up interview with Dorothy Stargazer about her missing aunt and uncle. And she had started working up a profile of Wild Willie Wellington. As Penny's editor somewhat callously put it, Dr. Pendergast was dead and buried, time to move on to covering the new folks on the scene.

Aside from being anointed by Mary Alice Hegler as her successor, Dorothy Stargazer was highly qualified for the position. After earning a degree in Library Sciences at IU, Dorothy had worked for several years as a branch manager in the Burpyville Library System. What's more, she was Mary Alice and Ernst Hegler's adopted niece, the daughter of The Great Wizardini's former stage assistant.

Penny had picked up a rumor that Dorothy Stargazer might actually be more than that – Ernst's illegitimate daughter. She certainly had the same blue eyes. But Penny wasn't going there with her story. In the Midwest, family secrets tended to stay buried. A social courtesy, it seemed.

The false genealogy of the Hoople Quadruples (as they'd been affectionately called) was an exception, front page news from Indy to Istanbul. After all, they had been famous.

A more immediate story would have been to discover where Mary Alice Hegler and her brother were hiding. Not that they were on any Wanted List, but readers liked that kind of follow-up detail, a "reveal" her editor called it. You know: Whatever became of a favorite old movie star? What's a one-time child actor doing now? Where had pinup queen Betty Paige been hiding? Where was Jimmy Hoffa buried? That sort of thing.

Penny was convinced that Dorothy Stargazer knew the Heglers' whereabouts, but the woman showed no signs of spilling the beans. It would be a real coup for an investigative reporter to find out. She just hoped those nosy parkers who called themselves the Quilters Club didn't beat her to the answer. Those gals were certainly persistent!

Chapter Seven

Herbie the Invisible Morlock

Tilly had a one-sided conversation with her invisible friend there in the car as they drove back from Marengo Cave. According to Maddy's daughter, Herbie was 7-foot-tall, with heavy brows and thick jowls, a stocky fellow with brownish skin and ragged clothes. Except for the skin color, she could have been describing The Incredible Hulk.

As Tilly told the story, Herbie had not recognized the murderer of Dr. Jonathan Segal, but confirmed that the killer was indeed a Morlock. Everyone knows Morlocks live underground, so Herbie was not surprised to see this fellow creature standing there in the Pillared Palace portion of Marengo Cave. She explained that Herbie himself was from a subterranean enclave in Salem, Indiana, called Suicide Cave. It was named after a moonshiner who offed himself in the 1820s. Raised there in Salem, Herbie didn't know any of the Morlock residents of Marengo Cave.

She again described the Morlock who killed the professor: Big and brown with two glowing eyes. Herbie confirmed the description, she said.

Mark kept his attention fixed on the road, his face hiding the pain that his wife was so far off in La La Land. Beau sat silently in the backseat, uncomfortable hearing his daughter talk about the inviable giant sitting next to her. But Tilly's mother gently urged her along with the story, drawing her out word by word.

"I didn't actually see the creature strike – what was the professor's name? – Dr. Segal, that's it! – but I'm pretty sure he was still holding the rock in his big paw."

"The sheriff's men didn't find a rock with blood on it," Maddy pointed out.

Tilly shrugged. "I guess he took it with him, back into that Blowing Bat hole. That's where he went after he saw me. Just slid in like a fireman going down a pole."

"A bloody rock not being there at the scene of the murder was one reason the sheriff released you," affirmed her mother. "Either someone took it away or you tossed it down the crawlway, he reasoned. His men went back several yards into Blowing Bat Crawl, but didn't find anything. They plan to do a more thorough search tomorrow, lowering themselves all way down the Crawl to the third level. I'm told there's a stream down there."

"Maybe they will find the Morlock," smiled Tilly. "Herbie says there's no other way out except the crevice behind the bronze plaque. And we were standing right there. No one came our way. He's likely still down there."

She could have been describing a game of hide-and-seek rather than a murder.

~ ~ ~

Dinner that night at Hoople Mansion was a quiet affair. The British-born housekeeper – Marybelle Olsen – had held up the meal for them. Roast lamb shank with scalloped potatoes for most of the family; a Waldorf salad for Tilly, the vegetarian in the group.

Maddy's ditzy "aunts" – Hilda and Helga, the two surviving member of the Hoople Quadruples – were complaining about the delay. Hilda worried the lamb would be overcooked; Helga worried it would be cold. Predictably, it was just perfect, thanks to Mrs. Olsen overseeing the cooks with an iron hand. Even the crème brûlée dessert was properly burnt.

Elsa Grottman – the live-in nanny – had put the three younger Tidemore children to bed promptly at 9 o'clock. Mrs. Grottman had eaten earlier with the "terrible trio." Recently, she had moved into the Mansion, getting her own room in the Tidemore family wing. There was plenty of space in the 52-room castle. Mrs. Grottman didn't need the job; the woman's late husband had left her well fixed. He had invented the Reverse Slinky, a toy that climbs up steps. The royalties were adequate for her needs. She had started babysitting the children to give her something to do, but had come to love them as if they were her own. And with Tilly living in a fantasy world, they may as well have been.

Aggie and N'yen were sorely missed, but a college education was important. Their BFF Sissy Jackson had often joined the family for dinner. She'd been all but adopted as a member of the household. Her grandfather had served in 'Nam with Beau Madison. However, tonight Sissy wasn't there, busy rehearsing for Caruthers High's production of *West Side Story*. She was playing the part of Maria. Colorblind casting was the big thing this year.

"Pass the pepper," said Aunt Hilda. She liked her lamb well-seasoned.

"None for me," Aunt Helga spoke up. She had a taste for the bland.

"The lamb shank is excellent," Mark complimented Mrs. Olsen. He seemed to be avoiding any discussion of today's adventure at Marengo Cave. Having your wife accused of murder was unsettling to say the least.

46

"Mmm, delicious," agreed Beau. He too was avoiding any serious conversation in front of his daughter Tilly. Or the Hoople sisters. They tended to buy into Tilly's fantasies. Tonight, they had insisted a place be set at the table for Herbie.

Maddy was not to be deterred, the Quilters Clubber in her coming out. Miss Marple on steroids, Beau called it. "Does Herbie like his lamb shank?" she asked matter-of-factly.

"Oh, Herbie prefers bats," smiled Tilly. "He says fruit bats were plentiful in the cave where he grew up."

"I'm afraid we're fresh out of fruit bats," Marybelle Olsen rolled her eyes, standing at the sidelines while the others ate. "We might have some fruit – apples or oranges – in the kitchen. But no bats."

"Oh, that's okay. Herbie doesn't eat very often. He stores up fat like a hibernating bear. That's why he looks a little plump right now, not that he's ever been thin. I suppose you noticed."

"No, dear. We can't see Herbie," reminded her mother.

"Oh, that's right. I forgot that he's invisible to other people. Only I can see him. You probably think I'm crazy, don't you?"

Everybody at the table was quick to reply, "No ... not at all ... of course not ... certainly not!" But their responses weren't very convincing."

"Something else Herbie told me about that Morlock who killed the professor. That he wore boots. That's unusual for a Morlock, they usually go barefoot. But Herbie, being a Morlock himself, noticed the discrepancy. In my fright I must have overlooked that detail."

"Well, we'll have to share this information with Sheriff Barneswell," said Maddy. "The sooner he catches the killer, the better." But she was thinking, The sooner we catch the killer, the sooner the spotlight will be off you, Matilda Madison Tidemore. Despite all Maddy's logic with the sheriff, her daughter remained the Number One Person of Interest in the case.

"I'll have some of the crème brûlée," said Tilly. "Nothing for Herbie, thanks."

~ ~ ~

Later that night Maddy tiptoed downstairs to the library.

The Quadruplets' mother had been a patron of the arts, amassing a large collection of paintings – mainly oils by the Hoosier Group – as well as an array of Chinese sculptures and Japanese vases.

The late Mrs. Hoople had also accumulated an impressive library, the shelves brimming with rare volumes and first editions ... as well as a complete selection of Mary Roberts Rinehart romances (obviously a guilty pleasure).

Just as expected, Maddy found a first edition of H.G. Wells' *The Time Machine* in the fiction section. Based on an earlier short story titled "The Chronic Argonauts," the longer version had been serialized in *The New Review* in 1895. A hardback edition was published in May of that same year by Henry Holt and Company.

According to the story, the human race had evolved in the future into two distinct species: the leisure class becoming the ineffectual Eloi, while the downtrodden working class had morphed into the brutal, light-fearing Morlocks – ape-like troglodytes who live underground in darkness and come out only at night.

A silly concept, it was meant to be a commentary on "the increasing inequity and class divisions of Wells' era, which he projects as giving rise to two separate human species."

Herbert George Wells' inspiration? His mother had worked as a housekeeper "in a house with tunnels below, where the staff and servants lived in underground quarters."

Thumbing through the volume, Maddy absorbed the author's description of Morlocks. Morlocks are the villains of the story, terrifying creatures who reside in a subterranean world, feasting on the peaceful Eloi. Wells described them as "nauseatingly inhuman," "new vermin," and he "likens them to rats." They possess "characteristics of apes with little or no clothing, gray fur, and large eyes to compensate the darkness underground." They were about five feet in height.

Well, thought Maddy, her daughter had got a few things wrong. She had described the Morlocks as being brown, not gray. And her friend Herbie was over seven-feet-tall. Or so she said. And Morlocks did not eat bats; they preferred to feast on humans.

At least, the body of Dr. Jonathan Segal showed no signs of bite marks!

Chapter Eight

Batshit Crazy

"**B**lowing Bat Crawl," Lizzie Ridenour repeated the name. "Are there bats down there?"

This being Tuesday, the members of the Quilters Club had convened at the Quilting Heritage Museum for their weekly confab. The women were all working on Crazy Quilts, using up the stray pieces of fabric they had amassed throughout the year.

"Yes, that's how that part of the cave got its name," nodded Maddy. "In 1992, cavers spotted bats flying out of the crevice. The wind blowing out of it told them there was a massive passage down there that one no one had ever been in. It took them quite a while to break through, I'm told. They found a lower level of the cave with a running stream. And lots of bats."

"Vampire bats?" asked Bootsie, the most impressionable member of the group. Her imagination sometimes got out of hand.

"No, common ol' Indiana Bats," said Maddy."

"We have our own bats?"

"Kinda," answered Cookie, drawing on her eidetic memory, as if having a reference library inside her head. "The Indiana Bat is a medium-sized mouse-eared bat that lives in

Southern and Midwestern states. They are quite small, weighing only one-quarter of an ounce – that's about the weight of three pennies. Gray, black, or chestnut in color, they have a wingspan of 9 to 11 inches. They were listed as endangered in 1967 due to people disturbing hibernating bats in caves during winter, resulting in the death of large numbers. Many have died off from white-nosed disease."

"White-nosed disease?"

"That's a fungus called *Pseudogymnoascus destructans.* It colonizes a bat's skin. There's no known treatment. Millions die every year. It has been called the greatest threat to bats ever seen."

"Gee, you're smarter than Bill Nye the Science Guy," said Bootsie, truly impressed.

"Bill Nye knows his stuff. I'm only a parrot quoting facts I've seen in books or online."

"Still impressive," agreed Maddy.

Lizzie gave a confirming nod. "You've been like that since we met in grammar school. But it still amazes me. You're a genuine freak of nature."

Cookie Bentley frowned. "Should I take that as a compliment?"

"Absolutely," cut in Maddy, before Lizzie put her foot in her mouth. She wasn't always the most diplomatic person with words, her comments sometimes unfiltered. Cookie was indeed a "freak of nature," but that wasn't the way the mild-manner historian liked to think of herself.

"Only about a hundred people in the world have been diagnosed as having my condition," the blonde librarian pointed out. "I think that makes me a rarity, not a freak."

"That's what I meant to say," Lizzie backtracked. "That you're unique."

"So what can you tell us about the vic?" coaxed Bootsie, using the police jargon she learned from her husband. Vic meant victim. "Maybe that will give us a lead on the perp." Perp meant perpetrator.

Cookie shrugged, then went into her encyclopedia mode. "Dr. Jonathan Livingston Segal? He was a professor of biology at Northwestern University."

"That's where N'yen goes to school," blurted Maddy. "I wonder if he had any classes with Dr. Segal?"

"I doubt it," said Cookie. "He's majoring in astrophysics. Biology is a bit far afield."

"You never know," said Bootsie. "I'm sure he has some elective courses."

"We should give him a call," urged Lizzie. "Ask him."

"Okay," agreed Maddy. "But first, let's hear what else Cookie can tell us about Dr. Segal."

"Give me a sec to pull up all the info I have stored in my brain."

"Take your time," Bootsie tried to take the pressure off. "We're in no hurry. He'll still be dead tomorrow."

"No, I think I've got it all. Dredging my memory banks doesn't take a lot of time. Like sending an email through cyberspace. It's almost instantaneous. That is, unless I get a mental block. That happens now and then."

"So what did you come up with?" coaxed Lizzie, not interested in the workings of her friend's mental circuitry.

"Professor Segal specialized in troglofauna. That is to say, animals that live in caves."

"You mean like bears and rattlesnakes?" Lizzie turned a shade paler. She wasn't the outdoors enthusiast her husband Edgar was. Since retiring from the bank, he spent most of his time hunting and fishing and traipsing through the woods like a later-day Jeremiah Johnson. She preferred sitting at home stitching on a patchwork quilt.

"Not so much bears and rattlesnakes as salamanders and bats."

"That's the kind of creatures – besides Morlocks – that are found in Marengo Cave?" asked Maddy.

Cookie closed her eyes for a second, then said, "Pretty much. Marengo Cave contains many types of animal life. On the walls, you might find centipedes, cave beetles, spotted tail salamanders, and daddy long legs. However, mosquitoes, flies, spiders, cave crickets, fungus gnats, and bats prefer the ceilings."

"Dr. Segal was there to study the bats," Maddy pointed out. "To make sure there were no strains of coronavirus found in local colonies."

Cookie nodded. "Yes, there was a note on the IKC website – that's the Indiana Karst Conservancy – announcing that they were working on a joint project with the National Institutes of Health, the Indiana Department of Natural Resources, and Northwestern University to carefully sample the bat population for the COVID virus. They had just got started, working through the caves in the southern part of the state. There are thousands of caves throughout Indiana, but not all of them host bats. The project was set to sample less than a dozen sites."

"Just our luck Dr. Segal would choose to sample Marengo Cave the very day we were there," huffed Maddy, angry at the confluences of events. She didn't like this much attention on her daughter ... or having her accused of murder! Tilly might be a little off the rails, but she wouldn't harm a butterfly. Or a cave cricket.

"Did you see any other staffers?" asked Bootsie.

"Sure, there was the guide taking us through the Crystal Palace, the person in the gift shop who sold us the tickets, a couple of others. It's privately owned, you know."

Bootsie shook her head. "I meant did you see any others who were part of Dr. Segal's bat survey team. I assume he didn't work alone. I'd think it would be dangerous crawling around in tight crevices all alone."

Cookie had the answer. "The Marengo Cave website lists Safety Tips. One of them says, 'NEVER go caving alone. There should be at least three in the group, and one should be an experienced caver.' "

"So where was Dr. Segal's team while he was getting bashed on the head by a Morlock?" demanded Bootsie.

"Good question," said Maddy. "I didn't see anyone. And the Sheriff didn't mention any associates being there with the professor."

"Strange," said Lizzie. "Why don't you call N'yen and find out who to talk with about the late Dr. Segal's bat project."

"Let me find my iPhone," said Maddy, hunting through her bottomless purse. She was always misplacing that darned phone.

~ ~ ~

"Sure, I know Dr. Segal," confirmed Maddy's grandson. Vietnamese by birth, N'yen had been adopted by her son Bill and his wife Kathy. Do-gooders at heart, they ran a save-the-children non-profit in Chicago. While used to dealing with disadvantaged kids, Bill and Kathy hardly knew what to do with a boy who happened to have an IQ that would have made Einstein proud.

Admitted at 16 to Northwestern through its early-admittance program, N'yen was majoring in astrophysics. But even Brainiacs have to take the basic courses. "I had some sessions on statistical analysis techniques with applications in physics, astronomy, biology, and finance," he elaborated. "Dr. Segal taught the one on biology."

"You know that he's dead?"

"Yeah, the school made an announcement. Something about a caving accident."

"It was murder," stated his grandmother bluntly. "Somebody hit him in the head with a rock."

"Murder, wow! Does that mean the Quilters Club is going to get involved?"

"We already are. The family – me and your Grampy, your Uncle Mark and Aunt Tilly – was there at Marengo Cave when it happened."

"Did you see it happen?"

"Almost. Well, at least Tilly did. She saw the attacker."

"Wow! Who was it?"

"That's not so clear. That's what we're trying to figure out."

"Let me help, Grammy. Maybe I can do some sleuthing on this end. I sure miss when Aggie and I were helping you guys solve crimes."

"Okay, you're enlisted. Can you find out about this bat study he was involved in with the NIH? Who was on his caving team? Who was with him when he went down in Marengo Cave yesterday?"

"I'm on it." He paused. "Uh, is Sissy working with you?"

"She's here with us right now. I'm sure she'll get hooked in."

"Maybe Sissy could be my contact ... that is, if you don't mind."

"I'm sure it will be fine," she said before hanging up. Ah, young love, she thought to herself.

Chapter Nine

The Underground World

Marengo Cave is a limestone solution cave, same as Mammoth Cave in Kentucky. Approximately ninety-five percent of the world's caves are located in limestone strata. These caves are formed when carbonic acid dissolves the rock through a very slow drip-drip-drip process. Marengo is a fairly new cave in geologic terms. According to geologists, it began to form from acidic ground water moving along bedding planes in the limestone sometime between 700,000 and 1,200,000 years ago.

Call it a million years.

The park above the Marengo Cave covers 122 acres of forested hills and valleys. This includes a small cemetery. The cave itself is approximately 5 miles in length. It consists of drier upper level passages and two parallel underground rivers.

On her recent visit, Maddy had picked up a brochure in the cave's gift shop. She browsed over the splashy features: Natural Adventure Trips, it advertised. But it didn't give many details. So she turned on the family computer and Googled her way to the Marengo Cave website.

Sleepover in Cave, it advertised. There were four Night in Cave options. But how would you know? she asked herself. It was always "night" in a cave. No, that wasn't the right package.

Underground Adventure

Take a two-hour cave exploring trip into the undeveloped sections of the cavern by advance reservation only.

Hmm, that sounded more like it. Was Blowing Bat Crawl one of those forays into "undeveloped sections"? If the killer had escaped down that hole, he might have left some clues behind in his haste. No one had found the murder weapon yet. Had he dropped the bloody rock as he scrambled down the chute?

Maybe the Quilters Club should take a look for themselves, she told herself. She could sign them up for a special underground adventure. It required a group size of 6 to 20. The four women plus Sissy made five. And she'd bet N'yen would come home for the weekend if it meant going caving with Cecilia LaToya Jackson! That would make six, the minimum number for a group.

At $34 each, the admission would amount to a little over $200 – pin money for a woman with a $200-million trust fund. There was an advantage to being a Hoople, illegitimate love child or not.

Maddy moved her cursor to the screen's pull-down tab labeled Cave Exploring. There were several choices.

The Waterfall Crawl promised:

Get muddy with a buddy! This adventure begins with the Red Room ladder entrance into Marengo Cave's New Discovery. Hidden from visitors for more than one hundred years, this section of cave was discovered on June 6th, 1992.

Trudge through the "Valley of Lost Soles". Visit Stewart Spring, Indiana's 13th largest producing spring, from underground.

Then exit from the "Pig Pen" named for the slimy wet clay that you'll be covered in. Great, not so clean fun!

Scrolling further, she discovered there was also a **Beyond the Falls** tour. That sounded interesting.

You've been asking for it, and now you've got it! Our Waterfall Crawl tour is now being extended beyond the falls.

On June 14th, 1992, a huge discovery took place. Explorers dug and opened a crawlway leading into one of Indiana's largest underground passages.

This one of a kind tour has you crawling, wading streams, scrambling and climbing over a mountain of breakdown into Stewart Hall. This massive room measures approximately 350 feet wide and over 250 feet long with a ceiling height of approximately 60 feet.

If you're looking to go where few have gone before then this is the trip for you!

Sounded like those two took you down the Blowing Bat Crawl to the third level. Now all she had to do was talk her friends into climbing down a muddy, dark hole 200-feet underground.

Chapter Ten

The Ace Reporter

Penelope Heath had received the tip that the wife of the mayor of Caruthers Corners was a Person of Interest in a murder case down in Crawford County. This insider information, of course, came from Penny's new hubby. He'd heard about it from his boss, Chief Jim Purdue. And Jim heard about it from his wife Bootsie, who heard about it directly from Maddy at the weekly Quilters Club gathering.

She had phoned the story in to the *Gazette*, barely making the deadline for tomorrow's paper.

Penny decided to poke around a bit, see if there might be a follow-up story. But she had to be careful, for she didn't want to get Harry fired after he'd just been promoted to lead detective. It was clear Jim Purdue was grooming him to be the next police chief.

Harry had been on a fast track at the Burpyville Police Department when he moved over to the Caruthers Corners PD to be close to his widowed mother. But Mrs. Teague had passed away recently. With his marriage to Penny it would have been more convenient to move back to the Burpyville police, but that would have put him at the end of the line for becoming chief. Jim Purdue's upcoming retirement was his best bet for advancement, even though it was a much smaller department. Being a police chief was his dream job and here was a sure shot if he (or Penny) didn't mess it up.

Harry and his wife had had "the conversation" before tying the knot – the separation of her job and his. He'd passed along tips in the past, but that had to stop. That was another reason for him sticking with his current job; being that Caruthers Corners wasn't her main news beat, there was less here to interest her with his work.

Penny had nodded and said yes and held up her palm like swearing Scout's Honor. But she was crossing her fingers on the other hand. A good story was a good story. And her job was to share news with the public. Well, at least with *Burpyville Gazette*'s readers.

Like that old advice column in *Ladies' Home Journal* had asked: "Can This Marriage Be Saved?"

~ ~ ~

N'yen Madison had been doing some digging of his own. He reported his findings back to the Quilters Club through Sissy Jackson.

According to the school's Admin Department, Dr. Jonathan Livingston Segal was a tenured professor in the biology department in the Weinberg College of Arts & Sciences at Northwestern University. His concentration was Ecology, Evolution, and Conservation Biology. As a biospeleologist, he was a world-renown authority in troglofauna and stygofauna. He spent most of his off-campus time slogging around in damp caves. He had a special interest in bats – endangered Indiana Bats specifically.

It was no surprise that the Indiana Department of Natural Resources and the National Institutes of Health would reach out to him to help sample the bat population for any signs of COVID viruses. He was the expected "go-to guy."

For the project, Dr. Segal led a four-man team – people he had handpicked for the assignment. The members consisted of himself, his number two in the biology department, a virologist from NIH, and an expert caver from the Indiana Department of Natural Resources. All were considered spelunkers of the first order. Some said they were more comfortable below ground than above it.

Although jokingly called "The Four Albinos" (due to their pale skin from lack of sunlight), the group was officially known as Chiropteran Survey Team 27, responsible for sampling the bats of Indiana, Kentucky, and Ohio for signs of the virus.

The four members were:

- Jonathan Livingston Segal, PhD.
- Jason Carlyle Wiener, PhD.
- Benjamin Raymond Bartle, MD.
- Hugo Merriweather Marston, MS.

"And yes," said N'yen, "all were at Marengo Cave on the day Dr. Segal died. Regulations require at least three of the four be present for each site visit that involves deep caving. All of them signed in that day, according to the University."

"How come the other members of the Survey Team didn't come forward and talk with the sheriff if they were at Marengo Cave when Professor Segal died?"

"Dunno. I'm trying to get an appointment with Dr. Wiener to ask him that very question. But he hasn't returned any of my calls yet."

"Well, keep trying," said Sissy, holding her iPhone close to her ear with her shoulder as she typed his report on her MacBook Pro. It was a 2019 13-inch with a 1.7 GHz Quad-Core

Intel Core i7 processor. Her grandfather had given it to her for her 16th birthday.

"Will do. It's good to hear your voice, girlfriend."

"Girlfriend? Are we still going steady?"

"You bet. Unless you don't want to."

"No, I like having a boyfriend – even if he is off at college."

"I'm coming down this weekend. Grammy says we're going spelunking."

"We're doing what?"

"Caving – that's what it's called."

"Cool."

"I'm looking forward to seeing you."

"Ditto," she said.

~ ~ ~

When Maddy and the other Quilters Clubbers heard N'yen's report, they agreed that something wasn't right with the Survey Team's behavior. Who would leave a fallen comrade behind in a damp limestone cave?

"There's something highly suspicious about that," Maddy summed up everyone's thoughts.

"I think we should tell my husband Jim, so he can report this to Sheriff Barneswell," said Bootsie.

"Yes, this is important information," agreed Lizzie. "Something smells rotten in Denmark."

"You mean in Crawford County," corrected Cookie, always a stickler for facts.

"Wherever," Lizzie waved the response away, her red nails flashing in the fluorescent light. They matched her freshly coiffured hair.

"Hold on, I'll call Big Bear right now." Bootsie kept her husband's private number on her speed-dial. She called it her Hubby Hotline.

Z-z-z-z-z!

"Hello, dear," she started off before he could get a word in edgewise. "The Quilters Club has come up with a piece of information you might want to pass along to that sheriff down in Crawford County. That dead man wasn't there alone. He had three co-workers with him – and not one of them came forward. They just skedaddled back to Northwestern University leaving that professor behind as if he were a stranger. Maybe they killed the guy. You've gotta admit their behavior was pretty weird."

"Hmm, that is odd. I'll give Jake a call. How did you gals find out about this?"

"Maddy put N'yen on the case. He goes to Northwestern, as you'll remember – same school as the dead professor."

'Thanks for the tip. But the Quilters Club has to stay out of police business. I keep telling you that."

"Well, that's a fine thank you. We hand you the biggest clue so far and that's the appreciation we get?"

"Baby Bear, it's not even my case."

"Yes, but Maddy's daughter is a suspect –"

"– a Person of Interest," he corrected.

"You say tomato, I say suspect."

"Don't worry. This new info should take Tilly off the hook. The suspicious behavior of Dr. Segal's co-workers puts *them* in the hot seat. I'll pass this along to Sheriff Barneswell. And then I'll call Mark and give him the news."

"No need to say 'You're welcome,' " she said sarcastically before pressing the red button to end the call.

"*Hmmpf*," she snorted to herself. Asking the Quilters Club to stay out of police business was like asking them to quit sewing patchwork quilts. Just wasn't gonna happen!

Chapter Eleven

Purely Academic

N'yen waited patiently in the outer office of Professor Jason Wiener. After much wrangling, the boy had managed to get a 3 o'clock appointment with the new head of the Biospeleology Department. Busy taking over the reins from the late Dr. Segal, he wasn't scheduling any meetings with students, but N'yen Madison's request had caught his attention. It said:

> I know you were with Jonathan Segal when he died. Talk with me about it or I will tell the police what I know.

A bluff. But it got him in the door.

"Well, young man, your note was quiet provocative," huffed Dr. Wiener. "I'm curious what you think you know. It sounded almost like a threat."

"Not at all," replied N'yen as he took the large chair in front of the professor's cluttered desk. "My aunt discovered Dr. Segal's body. She asked me to speak with you about it."

"Oh?"

"Everyone seemed to think Dr. Segal was in the cave alone. But rules are that all cavers must be accompanied by at least one other person. In the case of the Chiropteran

Survey Team 27, your rules require three of the four members being present for an excursion into a cave. So who else was there with Jonathan Segal."

"We all were – me, Benny Bartle, Hugo Marston. Business as usual."

"How come you haven't reported that to the sheriff in Lawrence County?"

"He hasn't asked."

"Maybe he doesn't know."

"I would have thought the Marengo folks would have told him. We have to sign in with each visit. Then we're left to go about our business, no staff guide or anything like that."

"Did you see my aunt in the cave?"

"We didn't see anyone. Arrived early that morning, slid down the chute at Blowing Bat Crawl, checked some bats, then left right before lunch. Missed all the tourists."

"If you guys finished your work and left, what was Dr. Segal doing there alone?"

"Beats me, kid. Now get out of my office or I'll report you to the Dean for harassing me. I'm going to check in with that sheriff down in Marengo and make sure he knows the facts. Then I've got a Biospeleology Department to run. Too bad about Jon Segal, but this is my Big Opportunity. They'll have to give me tenure now."

~ ~ ~

Everybody else was making Crazy Quilts, but Sissy Jackson had embarked on her greatest needlecraft challenge to date – a Shooting Star Quilt. This one is tough because it requires sewing triangles with odd angles.

Needless to say, Lizzie finished her quilt first. The others were making good progress, but Lizzie was fast. The Crazy

Quilt is one of the oldest quilt patterns. Early quilters used any scrap or remnant available, regardless of its color, design, or fabric type.

Now freed up, Lizzie helped Sissy with her Shooting Star. She showed the girl how to backstitch. Backstitching is done by sewing backward and forward at the beginning and end of a seam, on top of the seam stitches, to prevent the stitching from coming undone.

"There's no need to use a backstitch when making your quilt top," explained Lizzie. "About the only time I use a backstitch is to attach the binding to ensure a secure finish."

Binding is the piece of fabric that wraps around the raw edges of the quilt, the frame so to speak. This is the final step in making a quilt. "Because binding plays a crucial role in a quilt, you definitely don't want the stitches to unravel," explained Lizzie. Stating the obvious. "Back-stitching is used at the beginning and end of the fabric, as well as on each corner of the quilt."

Lizzie showed the girl her stitching technique: "Create a knot and insert the needle through the back of the fabric. Go back through the fabric from the front to create the first stitch. Bring the needle to the front again, leaving a space the size of the next stitch. Go through the end of the last stitch and repeat the process."

"You can speed it up a little by bringing the needle in and out of the fabric in one motion," added Cookie.

"When you get to the end, tie off the thread at the back," Lizzie completed the demonstration. The Quilters Club did all their sewing by hand, eschewing electric sewing machines. "Unplugged," they jokingly called it.

"I like to use a one-stitch backstitch as a lock on the stitch line," said Bootsie. She was the most unsure of her sewing among them. "I feel better with a single backstitch in what will be the seam allowances. I've had stitching pull out from time to time and got tired of having to mend the line during assembly or when pressing."

"Girls, I don't mean to be a Debbie Downer," interjected Maddy Madison. "But I'm worrying about Tilly. Innocent people sometimes get railroaded when law enforcement has no other suspects or there's conflicting evidence."

"Jim would never do that," protested the police chief's wife.

"We know that," said Maddy. "But this isn't Jim. We're dealing with a small-town sheriff on the other end of the state. He may be a super-dooper Walt Longmire – or not."

"And things like that *do* happen," Cookie piped up. "According to *The Chicago Tribune*, the rate of wrongful convictions in the United States is estimated to be somewhere between two percent and ten percent."

"See?"

Cookie added, "In addition to bad police work, the *Trib* cites bad prosecutors, false confessions, and inexperienced lawyers. As well as flaws in the Criminal Justice System."

"Now you're scaring me," shuddered Maddy.

"We've got to do something," said Lizzie. "Like find some evidence of Tilly's innocence."

"I'm sure Sheriff Barneswell's men have already scoured the crime scene," sighed Bootsie. She had a lot of confidence in the men in blue.

"Maybe not," said Maddy. "The murder took place in a dark cave. And right in front of a passageway – a narrow crevice where you have to crawl on your belly to get down to the level below. Since none of our tour group saw the killer coming or going, that must be how he escaped, disappearing into Blowing Bat Crawl like a rat down a hole."

"Is there a back exit?"

"No, but he might have snuck out after all the excitement was over. That third level extends over three miles back into the mountain. The sheriff's men didn't go looking all way back there. That would require expert cavers, not a couple of off-the-street deputies."

"Do you think the killer might have left a clue down there?" asked Lizzie. Eyes wide with excitement.

"That's possible," admitted Bootsie. "They never found the murder weapon, the rock or club or whatever was used to bop him on the head. Maybe the killer dropped it or stashed it down there in that lower passage."

"We've gotta go look," Sissy spoke up.

"My thoughts exactly," nodded Maddy Madison. "That's why I've bought us tickets to go on Marengo's Adventure Caving Tour this weekend."

"I knew that," smiled Sissy. "My boyfriend told me he's coming down to go with us."

Chapter Twelve

Penny on the Prowl

Having more or less eloped, Harry and Penny Teague decided to take a quickie honeymoon – a long weekend. Neither had much vacation time due, so it had to be some place close.

Penny made the selection, a four-star establishment called Hotel French Lick Springs. Located in Southern Indiana, it boasted four restaurants and two bars in addition to golf courses, tennis and basketball courts, as well as two swimming pools and a health club.

The resort just happened to be 40 minutes from Marengo. She wanted to take a look at that cave where the professor had been killed. She smelled a story here somewhere.

Penny was stretching it a bit, investigating a murder in a small town 250 miles to the south of Burpyville. As the new crime reporter for *Burpyville Gazette*, her beat technically didn't extend outside the county. Coverage was mostly Burpyville and nearby Caruthers Corners. If she stretched it, the paper's distribution area might include Berne, Geneva, and Decatur. But certainly not Marengo, a small town down in Southern Indiana edging up to the Kentucky border.

But the fact that the wife of the mayor of Caruthers Corners had been involved kinda made a legitimate connection. It certainly intrigued her. And everybody – even her pain-in-the-butt publisher – said she had a nose for news.

French Lick Springs was billed as "A Classic American Hotel." Built in 1845, with its spa wing added in 1901, the resort had "something everyone can enjoy, whether it's golf, spa, bowling, hiking, biking, swimming, or shopping." There was even a casino.

The seven-story hotel features 443 non-smoking rooms with a going rate of about $265 per night. Pricey for this part of the country, but worth every penny.

Harry was fine with the choice. And even at that price, it was a lot cheaper than a honeymoon in the Bahamas or Niagara Falls. Little did he know his wife's ulterior motive. He was expecting a weekend of newlywed bliss, not crawling around in the muddy depths of some damp, bat-infested limestone cave.

~ ~ ~

Aggie Tidemore was peeved when she found out that N'yen and Sissy were going off this weekend with the Quilters Club to search for clues in Marengo Cave. She didn't like being left out. What's more, it was *her* mother who'd nearly been arrested for the murder of some professor who was trying to catch bats.

But Yale University was a little too far away to pop home for the weekend. N'yen had an advantage. Northwestern was only 215 miles from Caruthers Corners, while Yale was a whopping 725 miles away. A bus ride versus an airlines flight and then some.

"Can you set up your Go-Pro camera so I can tag along visually?" she asked her cousin.

"Don't be daft. A cave is too dark for a video hook-up."

"Says online that the paths are well lighted," she retorted.

"That's for the regular tours. We're going off the grid, crawling on our bellies down a hole to the lower level. No lights down there except for our flashlights and headlamps. But Sissy and I will tell you all about it."

"Maybe we could Facetime on our iPhones?"

"There won't be a signal 200-feet under a mountain of limestone rock. But we'll call you afterward."

"Promise?"

"Promise."

"Keep your eye open for clues. And keep your mind off Sissy. This is not a Tunnel of Love."

"Ha! You won't be there to know what happens in the dark, Aggie Tidemore."

"Did I ever tell you, you are a rat? You belong down in a dirty old cave."

"Aw, you're just jealous cause the rat always gets the cheese – in this case being on hand to help solve another murder mystery."

"Hey, I'm part of the Quilters Club too. And I even know how to make quilts."

N'yen laughed. "Go solve the mysteries of the Skull and Bones, cousin. I got this one."

~ ~ ~

Mark Tidemore sat across from Tilly's shrink following her weekly session. Dr. Eichmann Fogle was explaining her schizophreniform disorder. "Your wife's malady is similar to that of Brian Wilson of the Beach Boys. He started having auditory hallucinations at the age of 22. Matilda started experiencing visual hallucinations around 36. Despite her fantasies, there's no reason she can't function in the real world. Brian Wilson still goes on tour, performing about 100 dates each year. I think we simply have to adjust her meds a bit. Perhaps that will do away with her imaginary companion, this so-call Morlock.

"Are imaginary companions common?"

"Not so much with adults. But that's definitely one of the symptoms of her schizophreniform disorder."

"Oh?"

"According to the American Psychiatric Association, an imaginary companion is defined as 'a fictitious person, animal, or object created by a child or adolescent' – in this case, an adult. 'The individual gives the imaginary companion a name, talks to it, shares feelings, pretends to play with it, and may use it as a scapegoat for his or her misdeeds. The phenomenon is considered an elaborate but common form of symbolic play.' "

"Symbolic play?"

"That's a form of play in which the child uses objects as representations of other things. For example, a child may put a leash on a stuffed animal, take it for a walk, and attempt to feed it. Symbolic play may or may not be social. In Tilly's case it may be a surrogate for her own thoughts and actions."

"Do you think she could have been responsible for that professor's death, then blamed it on one of her imaginary Morlocks? That is, used it as 'a scapegoat for her misdeeds.' "

"Possibly, but I doubt it. She shows no signs of aggression or violence. I would speculate that she witnessed something that she translated into her imaginary world and the characters that reside in it."

"So you think she did see the murderer?"

"It's quite probable. Maybe he was a big man with characteristics that she translated into the appearance of her Morlocks."

"Is there any way to unlock that memory – translate it back into the real world?"

"Hmm, hard to say. Hypnotism might work. But that's beyond my skills. I'm afraid I didn't take that course in med school."

"Where would I find one?"

"A hypnotist? Perhaps through law enforcement channels. They use them occasionally. But choose carefully. We don't want someone who does more harm than good. No stage magician or charlatan."

That made Mark Tidemore think of The Great Wizardini.

~ ~ ~

Ernst Hegler's stage name referred to his magical prowess –ranging from card tricks to slight-of-hand legerdemain, rabbits pulled out of hats to disappearing acts, sawing women in half to a mind-reading act, the Chinese water escape to hypnotism.

Although the stage hypnotism was more of the "quack like a duck" variety, Hegler was formally trained as a hypnotherapist.

The Great Wizardini had been a legendary act throughout the Midwest, but he was now retired. He'd been living with his sister in Caruthers Corners till she had been involved in the death of Dr. Henry Pendergast. That was when the old necromancer pulled his greatest disappearing act of all.

Chapter Thirteen

Adventure Tour

"Dark, wild worlds beckon explorers," an article in the *Baltimore Sun* noted. "The underworld just below our feet is attracting more people who want to taste the excitement of discovery ...

"Every year, millions of people enjoy the paved walks, colored lights and intricate formations of developed caves. For most, that's plenty. But others hear the call of the subterranean wild. Peering into unlighted side passages, they wonder about the dark, silent world beyond the lights – until recently, the private domain of experts ... equipped with special suits, ropes, climbing hardware and sometimes diving gear.

"Lately, rising demand has persuaded commercial caves to offer adventure tours for the speleo-curious ... However, the sport is not for the claustrophobic."

"I don't want to go," said Lizzie when her friend Maddy suggested the caving trip. "I don't like tight places. Besides, I could break a nail or something." Lizzie Ridenour was fastidious about her looks, with a standing appointment each week at the Helen of Troy Spa and Beauty Salon.

"You gotta go," urged Bootsie. "I need the moral support. I'm the one likely to get stuck in some narrow crawlspace. My diet just isn't working."

"The risk of dying in a cave is quite low," said Cookie. "Only 1 in 30,000. Since 1994, an average of 6.4 people have died each year in cave-related accidents in the US," she cited the statistics. "More than half of those deaths involved cave divers. And we're not going to be diving underwater."

"Aren't there underground rivers in Marengo Cave?" asked Bootsie. Not convinced.

"Two rivers," said Sissy. "But they're not deep." She had Googled the cave's website.

"Don't be overly dramatic," Maddy reassured her friend. "Worst that can happen is you'll get your feet wet."

"And muddy," whined Lizzie. "I don't like muddy. And I just got my hair done yesterday. I don't want to muss that up."

"I'll pay for a new appointment at Helen of Troy," offered Maddy.

That largesse irked her friend. As heir to the Bergamachi banking family, Lizzie was the largest stockholder in Caruthers Corners Savings & Loan. "This has nothing to do with money," she huffed. She didn't like being made to appear cheap. "This is a matter of personal care, hygiene, and looking good."

"You'll be inside a dark cave," Sissy laughed. "No one will be able to see your hairdo."

"Young lady, I can decide for myself," the redhead snapped. Then, lifting her chin, she declared, "Count me in. A little dirt won't kill me."

Nobody thought she believed that. Nonetheless, they patted her on the shoulder and said, "Way to go!" and other encouraging remarks.

Bootsie still wasn't convinced. "I wonder if my life insurance policy pays off on cave deaths?"

Sissy Jackson commented, "Down South we have Burial Societies. If I die it'll see that I get buried."

"Nobody's going to die," Maddy repeated patiently.

"Oh, I'm not worried," smiled Sissy. "I'm gonna carry five recipe cards from my dead grandma for good luck."

"That's silly," said Lizzie. "Recipe cards?"

"Yessum, that's a sure defense against Kin of Kudzu. Those are wandering spirits. I s'pect you might encounter them in a cave."

"You think recipe cards will protect you?" said Bootsie. More of a proponent of pistols and burglar alarms.

"Oh, that's not all," replied the girl. "I got me a gold tooth wrapped in wax paper tucked in a Folger's coffee can sitting on the back of a white shelf in a closet near the back door. That should be enough to protect the lot of us."

"Now I feel better," said Bootsie. Pause: "– not."

Chapter Fourteen

The Great Wizardini

"It's worth a try," agreed Police Chief Purdue as he and the Mayor climbed the stone steps of the Perricock Museum of Science & History. But their interest was neither science nor history. They were headed to the new library, a well-stocked bibliothèque that would have made a town twice this size proud, thanks to a generous grant from Maddy Madison's foundation. The library occupied an entire wing of the large museum.

"Have you ever used hypnotism to solve a case before?" asked Mark Tidemore.

Chief Purdue laughed. "Are you kidding? You oversee the Police Department's budget. We can barely afford a dispatcher, much less some kind of trained shrink."

"You have *two* dispatchers," Mark reminded him.

"But no staff psychologist. Or anyone trained in hypnotism. Just a handful of deputies adept at writing parking tickets."

"That's why we're going to see Dorothy Stargazer."

"True," he nodded. "Do you think she'll cooperate?"

"Maybe. She likes Tilly. And as the head librarian, she knows Tilly's Mom funded the purchase of all the books on her shelves."

"Yes, but you know she'd do anything to protect her uncle and aunt."

"Uncle, my left foot."

"You know what I mean."

"That's why I brought you along, to assure her that no criminal charges against Ernst Hagel or his sister Mary Alice will be forthcoming."

Chief Purdue removed his cap as they entered the library. "Guess I can do that," he said, running his hand over his slick dome. His hair seemed to recede more each year. "Judge Cramer said he will cooperate as long as it has your backing."

"I think she will believe you, Jim. You're a public official."

"So are you."

"Then we've got double the chances to convince her."

"Let's hope so – for your wife's sake."

"Also to help your colleague down in Crawford County solve a crime. Justice served, et cetera, et cetera."

"Yeah, that too."

The museum's entry was as large as a ballroom. To the left was the Science Museum wing, to the right the Historical Society. Nodding at the receptionist, the two men walked straight ahead through the double doors into the Library.

The building was even more massive than the Hoople Mansion next door. When Capt. Percival Perricock still lived here, it had been listed in the Guinness Book of World Records as the largest US home occupied by a single person. That was before Capt. Perricock moved to a rest home down near Indy and signed this big stone monolith over to the town.

Mark and his police chief stood patiently before the library's check-out counter, waiting for Dorothy Stargazer to come from the stacks, a hidden area where rare books, back issues of magazines and newspapers, off-limit volumes, and research material are kept. It was what's known as "closed stacks," with no entry to the general public.

"Oh, I'm so sorry," said Dorothy, breezing up to the counter. "No one told me you gentlemen were out here."

"Sorry to show up so unexpectedly," said Mark the Shark. "But I have a favor to ask."

"How could I say no to the mayor?" she smiled. Leaning against the counter as if swooning. You'd think she had a crush on him.

"It's a Big Ask,"

"Anything." She batted her eyes to confirm her willingness to help the son-in-law of the library's largest patron.

"Are you sure?" persisted Mark.

"Yes, *any*thing. You're my boss, after all."

"Will you put me in touch with The Great Wizardini?"

"No," she said.

~ ~ ~

Tilly had just spent $512.38 on assorted crystals at Rocket Power over in Burpyville. She had decided to encircle her king-size canopy bed with magical gemstones to protect her and Mark from incubi and succubi and other night-visiting demons.

Aunt Hilda and Aunt Helga had tagged along, fascinated by Tilly's new hobby. Maybe they would buy a few crystals for luck. Never hurts to try something new, they told each other. Especially if it might improve one's good fortunes.

Not that these wealthy old ladies needed any improvement to their fortunes. Being a Hoople Quadruple had paid off well over the years – even if they were fakes.

People had paid to see them; the money had been wisely invested.

The shopping went fast, the clerk stacking the selections next to the cash register. A pile of rocks grew on the surface of the wooden counter.

From the various bins, Tilly had picked out an obsidian sphere and several orange calcite points for Calm; a pyrite cluster for Courage; two rainbow fluorite points for Purpose; a sodalite rawpoint for Opportunity; an amethyst point for Intuition; and a dozen rose quartz points for Love. You couldn't have too much Love, she reasoned.

In addition, Tilly bought a Dream Decoder. She'd been having weird dreams lately, rambling adventures that involved Herbie, an incubus (or was it a vampire bat?), and a unicorn. Once she'd dreamed she was naked on-stage at the high school, standing there in the middle of a musical version of Shakespeare's *As You Like It*. Somehow it involved a crow and a cockatoo, the two of them singing "Old Man River" as a duet.

With that in mind, Tilly asked if they had some crystals that might help her sleep better.

"Fluorite and green calcite offer a calming and soothing energy that will put you at ease after facing a long day," suggested the clerk, a cousin of Margie Yost. Margie owned the nearby Helen of Troy Beauty Salon. She also had a controlling interest in Rock-et Power.

"That's exactly what I need," gushed Tilly, adding more purchases onto the rock pile next to the cash register.

"I'll take some too," tittered Aunt Hilda.

"Me too," nodded Aunt Helga. "I've never bought rocks before."

While Tilly was at it, she selected a T-shirt that said:

PEOPLE WHO LOVE CRYSTALS
HAVE ROCKS IN THE HEAD!

Tilly thought the message was somewhat pejorative. But she bought the T-shirt because Herbie said he liked it.

Chapter Fifteen

Tunnel Rat

Maddy bumped into Buck Jackson at Food Lion. Marybelle Olsen usually did the grocery shopping, but Maddy had volunteered to pick up some romaine lettuce for tonight's Caesar salad on her way home from the Quilting Heritage Museum. The Tristan and Isolde Quilt Exhibition was nearly ready for the public.

"Oh, hi there, Buck," she greeted her husband's old Army buddy. "I was planning to call you this afternoon."

"Well, this saves you a phone call. What can I do for you, Maddy?"

"I wanted your permission to take Sissy caving with us on Saturday. N'yen is coming home to go with us down to Marengo."

"Didn't you just go down there? Word is you folks stumbled on a dead college professor."

"That's true. Now we're going back to look for clues."

"Clues to what?"

"We think Dr. Segal was murdered. We're looking for the rock he was hit on the head with. The sheriff's deputies didn't find it."

"Oh, the Quilters Club rides again."

"Something like that."

"I'm sure my granddaughter will be safe with you gals. But you couldn't pay me to go down in that hole."

"Why's that? Are you claustrophobic?"

"Naw, it's just that I spent part of my time in 'Nam as a Tunnel Rat. We had t' go down in what we called Spider Holes to flush out them gooks ... no offense to your grandson N'yen, he's a mighty fine boy. I think my Sissy is sweet on him."

"Is that all right?"

"Sure, they make a fine young couple. But over in 'Nam them Viet Cong were shootin' at us. Soldiers in black pajamas were hiding down in them tunnels with AK-47s and mortars. When you crawled down in one of them tunnels, you never knew which one of you was coming out."

"Did Beau go down in those – what did you call them? – Spider Holes?"

"No, that was before I met 'im. Before I became a sergeant. At that time I was just an expendable grunt the looies used like a human roto-rooter. Our motto was *Non Gratus Anus Rodentum.*"

"What does that mean?"

"Don't ask. Ain't polite words for a lady. We Tunnel Rats had a casualty rate of 33 percent, high even by Vietnam War standards. Lucky I survived!"

"That's horrible."

"Give you one tip I learned from going into them tunnels. Take a compass with an illuminated dial. You get lost, that'll help you get out. Other trick is a ball of string, but I hear Marengo Cave is mighty long, so it would take an awful big ball of string to make a guideline to follow."

"Anything else?"

"Kneepads. Them rocks are hard on kneecaps when you're crawling around on all fours."

~ ~ ~

Tilly was unpacking her purchases from Rock-et Power, a glittery collection of odd-shaped stones. She was confident that these would assure her happiness, calmness, etc. She was very pleased with her haul.

She and her aunts had come directly home from Burpyville, having enjoyed the outing together. The three women shared a childlike view of the world, drawing them closer in recent months.

Tilly and Herbie had retreated to her suite to sort the rocks. Aunt Helga went to her studio to work on a painting – a dog, a wolf, a coyote, some kind of canine creature from her sketchbook. Aunt Hilda took the Rolls out again, running an errand.

Being a Morlock, Herbie liked pretty rocks. He encouraged her interest in crystals. Apparently, his species was big on Crystal Power. It ran their underground machinery.

Tilly wasn't sure what the Morlock machinery did, something about providing food and clothing, pumping air, keeping the world turning on its axis. Herbie was always vague about this part.

Sometimes she wondered if Herbie was real or only a figment of her imagination. It didn't really matter. She didn't distinguish between real and imagined. When she saw the movie *The Matrix*, she questioned whether Neo was plugged into an AI-induced fantasy ... or the AIs were his fantasy.

They say there's a thin line between genius and madness. She was feeling very smart lately. And Herbie agreed.

Chapter Sixteen

The Bad Prognosis

Hilda Hoople left Doc Medford's office in a huff. Dr. Franklin Delano Medford had just shared the results of a biopsy. Miss Hoople had tested positive for cancer. It was back!

The erstwhile Hoople Quadruplet had had a scare about ten years ago, an indication of ovarian cancer that had resulted in a hysterectomy. No problem in that. She'd been well beyond the child-bearing age. This lack of children had been part of the motivation to accept Maddy Madison as her "niece," set up a trust fund for her "brother's" biological daughter, and move the entire Madison clan — well, Maddy and her husband, Maddy's daughter Tilly and her family — into the empty old mansion she called home.

When her "sister" Helga had turned up alive, she had been invited back also. A so-called haunted house had turned into a lively, bustling household with children and staff and a delightful sense of chaos. It had been the best thing Hilda had ever done.

Now the Big C was back.

Or so the biopsy said.

But Hilda wasn't ready to accept that bad news. A trip to the Mayo Clinic would follow, she decided. She'd get a second

– maybe even a third – opinion, as if finding a dissenting voice would make the condition go away.

But in her heart, she knew the end was nigh. Doc Medford had given her three months.

"How did it go," asked Helga Hoople. Helga had finished her painting of a wolf. She liked wildlife and such. But her painting was pretty amateurish.

"Fine," Hilda lied. "Everything was perfectly fine."

"That's good. Let's go down to the Cozy Café for tea."

"Maybe scones too?"

"Marybelle makes better scones."

"Maisie tries. Besides, she's our niece too – Maddy's twin sister."

"Lordy, our genealogy chart was surely a mess," said Hilda, putting the big car into gear. It moved forward with a lurch. Driving was never her strong point.

"Yes, but we've finally got it straightened out," said Helga. "We have a fine family now."

~ ~ ~

Cozy Café was a typical small-town diner, with a silvery aluminum front and a neon sign in the window proclaiming that it was **OPEN**. A counter ran along the back of the restaurant with padded stools fronting the red Formica top. Condiments – ketchup, mustard, salt, pepper, and a napkin holder – were grouped along the counter as well as on each of the tables. The tables were fewer these days, thinned out to provide social distancing. Even though the entire town had been inoculated with the 95%-effective Mod-Tim vaccine, everybody still wore masks around town in an abundance of caution.

Owner Maisie Walters had discovered she was a separated-at-birth twin, the scion of Hebert Hoople. This fact earned her a fat trust fund that would have allowed her to retire comfortably to her own mansion, but she preferred to continue her life in modest style, still running her little café as a community gathering place.

Cozy Café was known for its "Endless Cup of Coffee," still only 50¢. Nonetheless, she never hesitated to set a pot of Darjeeling tea boiling whenever she saw the Hoople sisters – her "aunties" – step through the café's revolving door.

"Welcome, Aunt Hilda, Aunt Helga," she greeted the two dotty old women. "I've just put on a pot of tea. Be ready in seconds. Pastries? Cookies?"

"Scones, thank you," said Aunt Hilda.

"Shall we take that table in the corner?" asked Aunt Helga.

"It's yours," said Maisie with a wide smile. Being only a fraternal twin, she and Maddy looked nothing alike. Maddy exuded the style and dignity of that actress Ellen Burstyn; while Maisie reminded you more of an aging Flo from those Progressive Insurance commercials.

"Hilda was just at the doctor's," blurted Helga. "We thought a cuppa tea would be a nice way to celebrate a clean bill of health."

"Yes, everything was perfect," lied Hilda. "As good as an eightysomething-year-old antique could expect." The second statement closer to the truth.

"Wonderful," said Maisie, ushering them to their corner table. Most customers didn't get the maître d' treatment, but these old women were family.

While Maisie was serving the tea and scones (little did they know that their housekeeper Marybelle baked these scones for the diner in their very own kitchen at the Mansion), the moment turned somber. "Maisie, I want you to hear this," said Aunt Hilda. "Something I've been thinking about for a long time."

Yes, like about fifteen minutes.

"What's that?"

"We're getting older. No need to wait till the end. I plan to ask Barney to divide up the Hoople Quadruplets Foundation among the entire family – you and Maddy, children, grandchildren, everybody. Even a nice contribution to the town's coffers. I don't know what Hilda wants to do, but I'd urge her to do the same. Let us spend our remaining years without the headaches of wealth."

Barney was, of course, Barnabas Soltairé, the high-powered lawyer who managed the Foundation. He'd grown up in the Hoople household, his mother a lifelong maid there. He'd get a share too.

"If we gave everything away, where would we live? How would we feed ourselves?" asked Helga. Always a little insecure.

"We wouldn't be relying on the kindness of strangers ... we'd be relying on the kindness of family. I expect Maddy would want us to stay on in the mansion just as we are. Marybelle would still oversee the cooks, giving us meals. I doubt our day-to-day life would change very much."

"Wow!" said Maisie. "Are you sure about this?"

Aunt Hilda smiled, her face like crinkled parchment. "Nobody lives forever. Why not clean up everything in advance?"

"Well, if you think that's the thing to do, count me in," shrugged Aunt Helga. "We quadruples have shared the same fate most of our lives. Why stop now."

"Then it's settled. I'll call Barney this afternoon and tell him to put everything in motion."

Chapter Seventeen

The Prodigal Grandson

N'yen arrived on the 4 o'clock Trailways bus. Although 16, he still didn't have his driver's license. He carried a blue duffle bag with few items in it. Although his parents lived in Chicago, he had a permanent room – actually a suit of rooms – at Hoople Mansion, so he didn't need to pack much.

Aunt Hilda and Aunt Helga were delighted to see him, clucking over him like mama geese preening over a gosling. Marybelle Olsen had directed the cooks to make his favorite dish for dinner – Pho, a Vietnamese concoction consisting of a salty broth, fresh rice noodles, a sprinkling of herbs, and chicken.

Beau Madison – better known to N'yen as Grampy – and Uncle Edgar met him at the bus stop in front of Town Hall. They had been hoping he would go fishing with them this weekend, but his visitation had been preempted by the Quilters Club.

"Hi, Grampy," he called as he stepped off the Trailways. "Who's that hairy old Bigfoot behind you."

"Hey, watch who you're calling a Bigfoot," laughed Edgar Ridenour. "I got a haircut just six weeks ago." Since retiring from the bank, he'd let his beard and hair go wild. And he'd swapped his pinstriped suits and power ties for overalls and cammies.

"I'd recommend you fire your barber," the boy replied, fast on the uptake.

"Come along, everybody's waiting to see you." Beau Madison nodded toward the Rolls Royce. He'd borrowed the Hoople sisters' limo to pick up his grandson. Greeting the boy in style.

"Can I drive?"

"You don't have a license, young man. We don't want your Uncle Jim giving you a ticket."

"I've got my Learner's Permit," he announced. A major accomplishment.

"We'll save that drive for your next visit," said Beau. "And I think it would be better to use our old sedan. Not as expensive to repair as a Silver Cloud."

"Aw, rhubarb," the boy grumbled.

"Sissy Jackson's waiting for you at the Mansion," Edgar diverted the conversation. Knowing the boy's true interest.

"Say, that's great. Let's get going."

~ ~ ~

Mark had explained to Dorothy Stargazer that he needed to get in touch with her uncle. In addition to being a magician, The Great Wizardini was a hypnotist. He often used his mesmerizing abilities in his stage act, but his skills were real. He belonged to the American Hypnosis Association. And he had been certified by the American Society of Clinical Hypnosis. Technically, Ernst Hegler was qualified to be a clinical hypnotherapist, but he'd always preferred to use this know-how for entertainment purposes.

Only after impressing the librarian with the seriousness of the situation, along with Chief Purdue's assurance that neither Ernst Hegler nor his sister would be charged with a crime – the death of Henry Pendergast was closed – that she relented and agreed to pass a message to the old man.

Even at that, she refused to reveal where her uncle and aunt were hiding, merely saying The Great Wizardini would get in touch with Mark if he were willing to help.

Maybe Maddy Madison's patronage of the library had something to do with Dorothy agreeing to contact the two fugitives. Or maybe it was because she had always liked Mark Tidemore and his pretty wife. Or maybe Dorothy was just a kind and empathetic person.

Or maybe she saw this as a safe way for Ernst and Mary Alice to come out of hiding. Rehabilitation was the word that came to mind.

Chapter Eighteen

Sissy Puts Her Foot Down

"This relationship just might not work out," Sissy Jackson announced over dinner that night.

"Hey, why not?" squeaked N'yen, spilling his green tea all over himself, the result of the sudden discombobulation caused by her unprompted statement.

The conversation around the table came to a put-on-the-brakes halt.

"Because of this funny food you eat," Sissy replied. "A bunch of twigs and noodles. I'm not sure I could spend the rest of my life eating this stuff."

"But this is Pho, my favorite dish."

Sissy sighed. "My point exactly, N'yen Madison. Give me some good ol' comfort food – cornbread and ham hocks, meatloaf and mashed potatoes, macaroni and cheese."

"I like that kinda food too."

"Problem is, I don't know how to cook Goi Cuon and Rau Muong, or Cao Luo and Bun Cha. I'd be a bad wife for you."

N'yen laughed, "I'm impressed that you even remember the names."

"I make a pretty good meatloaf. But Pho –?"

"Don't worry about that," offered Marybelle Olsen. "If you two ever got married and moved into the Mansion, the cooks

93

could prepare anything you like – from cornbread to Banh Xeo." By now, Marybelle was like part of the family, free to enter into the dinner conversations.

"Lordy mercy," responded Sissy. "It's a little early to be talking about wedding bells. N'yen has only asked me to go steady. Ain't like we're engaged."

"I should say so," agreed Maddy. "You're both only sixteen. Barely old enough to be dating."

"Juliet was only thirteen," Marybelle reminded them. Being English, she was a big fan of the Bard. *Romeo and Juliet* was her favorite play.

"Things were different back in Shakespeare's time," argued Maddy.

"Oh posh," said Marybelle. "I was only seventeen when I got married to Reginald Olsen. Too bad he died so young – only 23 when I lost him."

"I'm so sorry to hear that," said Maddy.

"Yes, he was swallowed by a python. We lived in India at the time."

"Swallowed by a snake!"

"It was his own fault. Trying to feed it a candy bar. Leaned in too close."

"Well, N'yen and Sissy have no time to waste," exclaimed Aunt Hilda. "They had best get hitched before the boy's eaten by a Crab Nebula. Isn't that one of the creatures he studies in the sky?"

"More likely he will be swallowed up by a Black Hole," suggested Aunt Helga. "I've heard about them things. Like a giant vacuum cleaner in the galaxy."

"Yes, being an astronaut is a dangerous job. Flying to the Moon and all," nodded Tilly. "Do you have your own spaceship?"

"I'm studying to be an astrophysicist, not an astronaut," he corrected them. "Nothing dangerous about that."

"Even so, are you going to do right by this young lady or not?" Aunt Helga demanded. Like a surrogate parent concerned about an offspring's honor.

Sissy couldn't help but giggle.

"Hey, give me time. At the rate I'm going, I should be able to earn my Master's Degree in two more years. Then I can get a full-time job as an astrophysicist and support us."

"A job's not necessary," said Aunt Hilda. "We can set up a Trust Fund for you like we did for Agnes. Then you wouldn't have to work."

"My own Trust Fund?"

"Helga and I have decided to divide up our money between all of you – the entire family."

"Yes, a Trust Fund for every single one of you," added her sister. "Cecelia too if she marries you. It would be wonderful to have you and Cecelia around full time. You already have a suite here in the Mansion. We can turn everyone's living space into a condo, so you actually own your rooms."

"Aunt Hilda, Aunt Helga – what's gotten into you?" said Maddy, her fork poised in mid-air, a bite of chicken spiked on the tines, inches from her mouth. She wasn't very skilled with chopsticks.

"Not a thing at all," Hilda said hastily. "We just decided there's no need for you to wait until we are dead and gone before you get to enjoy the family fortune."

"We're already doing that."

"If we divided everything up," reasoned Helga, "N'yen and Cecelia could move in. Aggie could come home. We'd even have room for Bill and Freddie's families. No need for *any*body to work."

"But Bill and Kathy *like* running that children's shelter in Chicago. And Freddie *likes* being a fireman."

"What about your sister Maisie?"

Maddy shook her head. "She will never change her lifestyle, living in that small cottage, running the diner. She prefers to use her money for good deeds."

"But she could come live here in the Mansion. We still have unused rooms."

"Don't count on it."

"And Agnes?"

"Aggie is studying to become a lawyer. That decision is a few years away."

Aunt Hilda sighed. "Well, at least N'yen and Cecelia can join us here."

"But I like being an astrophysicist. I've already discovered a new quasar."

"We could convert the cupola off your bedroom into a professional observatory," insisted Aunt Hilda. "Add a big telescope and everything you need."

"Yes," nodded Aunt Helga. "Then you could look at stars all you like."

"We'd love to have Sissy as an official member of the family," added Tilly, picking at her chickenless version of Pho. "She could help me care for my unicorn."

"You don't have a unicorn, dear," said Maddy.

"I'd like to have one."

"We'll buy you one," said Mark, placating his wife.

"I think we all need to step back and take a deep breath," said Sissy, rolling her eyes. "I'm not ready to get married yet. No matter how young Juliet was."

"I agree," echoed N'yen. "Let's see how going steady works out. If we like it, then we can think about getting engaged. And then maybe get married someday."

"But what about that funny food –?" Sissy reminded him.

"Food's not an issue," said N'yen. "We could compromise on hot dogs, hamburgers, and pizza."

"Hm, I could live with that."

Chapter Nineteen

Appearing in a Puff of Smoke

"**A**bracadabra!" said The Great Wizardini as he miraculously appeared in Mark Tidemore's office the next day, a puff of blue smoke swirling around him like a Dust Devil.

"Hello Ernst," the mayor greeted his unannounced visitor. "Thanks for coming."

"Dorothy said you needed my assistance. Something to do with your lovely wife. She made a great assistant that time we brought your father-in-law back from the dead there at the bandstand in the Town Square."

"He wasn't really dead."

"I know that, you know that, but the audience didn't know that. That's the basis of all magic."

"As I told your niece, I need your help – as a hypnotist."

"This is not some kind of trap, is it?"

"No, of course not. Chief Purdue told Dorothy to tell you that you and your sister face no charges. You're free to come and go."

"You mean we could move back to Caruthers Corners?"

"We would be pleased to have you. Both of you."

"Bully. Dorothy has kept our rooms waiting. I put the house in her name before we left."

"Where have you two been hiding?"

"In plain sight. We've been renting a house in Wabash Acres. Dorothy brings us groceries. We haven't been outside even to check the mailbox. Dorothy does that for us too. Nobody notices our reclusiveness in this Age of Covid."

"About that favor ..."

"You want me to hypnotize Tilly, I take it?"

"Yes, if you think it's safe."

"Of course, it's safe. Hypnotism is merely the power of suggestion. I cannot make a subject do anything he or she is not willing to do."

"I heard that you're certified as a clinical hypnotist."

"True. I got my hypnotherapy certification from The American Society of Clinical Hypnosis. Located over in Bloomingdale, ASCH is the country's largest professional organization for mental health care professionals using clinical hypnosis. Their program requires two hypnotherapy training workshops, plus 20 hours of supervised individual training, and 2 years of practical experience using hypnosis as a part of your practice. In my case, my practice was my stage work. But they were willing to count it."

"What is the difference between hypnosis and hypnotherapy?"

"Although the words are used interchangeably, they are not the same. Hypnosis is more a state of mind while hypnotherapy is the name of the therapeutic program in which hypnosis is used."

"So exactly what does a hypnotherapist do?"

"By inducing a trance-like state in the subject, a hypnotherapist helps him or her use the subconscious mind to change behavioral patterns or ways of thinking. It's often used to cure smoking, help control eating disorders, treat allergies, or provide anesthesia for liver biopsies, upper GI endoscopies, and colonoscopies."

"What about mental diseases?"

"Like what?"

"Tilly's shrink had diagnosed her as having some kind of schizophreniform disorder."

"Schizophrenia is a serious mental disorder that can alter people's senses and change the way they understand the world. The symptoms vary depending on the individual. These can include delusions, hallucinations and illusions, disordered thinking. It can also cause social withdrawal. Or even total madness."

"You certainly know your beans."

"I got the certification, just never practiced."

"So what's the cure for schizophreniform disorder?"

Ernst Hegler shrugged. "No one knows for sure. But the malady is seen as a chemical imbalance in the brain. The primary treatment is usually antipsychotic medications. However, not everyone responds to these drugs. Other interventions include talking therapies, relaxation, and hypnosis. They have been applied with varying degrees of success."

"Would you be willing to try?"

"For Tilly, anything."

~ ~ ~

Barnabas Soltairé started the work required to dismantle the large and powerful Hoople Quadruplets Foundation. It was quite a task, for he had set up a byzantine financial structure to shelter their money. Not that it was needed, but as a former mob lawyer he was used to hiding wealth and ownerships and such.

Perhaps it was time to pack it in, he told himself. The old ladies were in their 80s, liable to drop dead with the next heartbeat. May as well do this in an orderly fashion rather than scrambling on a moment's notice.

Hilda and Helga had given him a formula for distributing their estate. Easier said than done. The idea was that Maddy and Maisie got the lion's share, Maddy's children got a lesser share, and her grandchildren each got a healthy chunk. Maisie had no problem with more going to Maddy's side of the family due to her three children and seven grandchildren; she loved them all as if they were her own.

No matter, Maisie would have more inheritance than she could spend in a lifetime. Her lifestyle was very frugal.

Maddy herself would get an equal amount as Maisie. She and Beau would be well provided for.

Bill, Freddie, and Tilly would have more than they knew what to do with. Bill would pour a lot into his NGO children's service. Freddie would likely buy the station another firetruck. Tilly would buy a unicorn, if Mark didn't control her impulses.

All the grandchildren already had college funds – thanks to Maddy. But this added more on top of that. Maddy worried about them being handed a bundle of money without having to earn it. She wasn't in favor of "trust fund babies," even if she was now one herself.

Barnabus himself would get a share equal to the Maddy and Maisie. He was as close to a son as Hilda or Helga would ever have. And Marybelle would get a healthy stipend.

The remainder would go to various charities – mostly those related to the Caruthers Corners community. Despite traveling around the world as children, Caruthers Corners had always been their home.

It reminded Barnabus of that Shirley Jackson book, *We Have Always Lived in the Castle*. An eerie tale ... but then again the Hoople Quadruples had led an eerie life, their genealogy chart as tangled as a ball of string.

He hoped all the beneficiaries would be able to maintain their sense of small-town life. Even though he lived in a plush penthouse atop one of the tallest buildings in Indianapolis, Barnabus Soltairé missed his childhood growing up in Caruthers Corners.

Chapter Twenty

"Look into My Eyes ..."

"**M**r. Hegler ... uh, I mean Great Wizardini, what are you doing here? I thought you and Mary Alice were on the ... on a vacation."

The old magician cracked a smile, a wide row of yellowing teeth that reminded one of a Halloween mask. "Vacation's over, my dear girl. Mary Alice and I are coming back to town. Mrs. Bentley is going to take her back as a researcher at the Historical Society."

Tilly beamed. "Oh, that's wonderful news. I've missed you two. I have so few friends here in the Magic Forest."

Ernst Hegler glanced at Tilly's husband, a look of concern flickering across his face, then quickly disappearing. "No need for concern, my dear. I've come to lead you out of the forest, to leave the demons and goblins and Morlocks behind."

"But what about Herbie?"

"Who?"

"Herbie, my Morlock friend."

"Herbie is homesick. He wants to return to the cave he came from."

"I knew he'd go back someday. I'm going to miss his company."

"You will have other company. Your daughters, for example."

"But Aggie is away on a magical quest. And the three pixies have their own mischief to make."

"Your daughters have been enchanted, turning them into pixies, but we will break the spell and restore them as little girls. You will enjoy being their mother again."

"Okay."

"Now just try to relax."

"Your voice sounds so soothing. It makes me sleepy."

"Yes, that's the idea. You must go to sleep ... on the count of three. One, you are getting very sleepy. Two, you cannot keep your eyes open. And three, you are sound asleep. But you can still hear my voice, can you not?"

"Yes, Great Wizardini."

"Now we are going to cast aside the spell put upon you, return you to the real world, leave the magical world of dragons and unicorns behind."

"As you wish."

"Here, take my hand and I will lead you out of the dark forest, guide you into the light. When I snap my fingers you will have left that magical world behind and rejoined your friends and family in the real world."

"Yes, into the light."

"Into the light," he repeated. "Are you willing to follow me?"

"Yes, Great Wizardini."

"When you hear me snap my fingers you will be released from the spell. Do you understand?"

"Yes, Great Wizardini."

"Three ... two ... one." The old man paused, then – *snap!* – he broke the spell.

~~ ~

Tilly Tidemore was sitting up in bed, a tray of tea balanced on her lap, looking over at her husband who was standing next to her. "I feel like I've been far, far away," she said as she nibbled on an orange scone. Mrs. Olsen had prepared the scones – "biscuits," she called them – especially for Tilly's so-called "homecoming."

"Glad to have you back."

"These are really good," Tilly said, holding up the half-eaten scone for her husband to see. "Want one?"

"I'm okay for now," he demurred.

"I've been having the weirdest dreams lately. All kinds of crazy stuff. I was in a mythical land that was like this one, but everyone I know was different. Kinda like in *The Wizard of Oz* when the Kansas farmhands turn into the Tin Woodman and his friends."

"Just your imagination at play," affirmed Mark. Not a shark at the moment. He was so relieved to have his wife back – even though he was unsure whether this recovery was temporary or permanent. But he owed the Great Wizardini his undying gratitude. The old stage magician sometimes defied the humbuggery associated with his profession. His skills as a hypnotist – actually, as a hypnotherapist – were impressive. His careful suggestions planted in Tilly's mind had led her back to the real world.

At least for now.

As Ernst Hegler had explained, he had no control over Matilda Madison Tidemore's underlying psychological problems or genetic disposition or the synapse misfires in her brain that had sent her on a journey to the edge of madness. But for today, Tilly was her "old self," a loving mother and wife who was happy to be back home.

Chapter Twenty-One

The Bat Hunter

"**N**obody hit him with a rock," stated Dr. Jason Wiener. "He banged his head on the roof of the cave. You may have noticed, Jon was pretty tall."

"So are you," noted the Sheriff. "Isn't that a liability for spelunkers?"

"It would appear so. But we didn't get picked for this assignment because of height. We were selected because of our knowledge about Indiana Bats. We've worked with the Department of Natural Resources before."

"And the NIH?"

"This is my first time. But Jon was a regular. So was the state guy, Hugo. He had an 'in' of some kind."

"I suppose you have a good excuse why you gentlemen left without bothering to even identify the body."

"Simple. We didn't know Jon was dead."

"You just up and left without checking on him? Wasn't he the team leader?"

"Exactly. We'd finished up. Time to go home. Hugo's wife was having a baby. Jon told us to go on ahead, he'd catch up. So we headed back to Evanston. That's where the Weinberg campus is located."

"Weinberg? I thought you were with Northwestern."

"The Judd A. and Marjorie Weinberg College of Arts and Sciences is the largest of the twelve schools comprising Northwestern University. It's located both in Evanston and downtown Chicago. The Biology Department itself is based in Evanston. That's where Jon and I were located."

"When did you learn of your colleague's death?"

"I got a call later that night from the Dean. The State Police notified him."

"You drove straight home from the crime scene?"

"I drove straight home from Marengo Cave. I didn't know it was a crime scene till about ten o'clock that night. Jon – Dr. Segal, that is – is going to be a great loss to the school. He has headed up the Biospeleology section of the Biology Department for going on ten years now."

"Bio – what?"

"Cave biology. It's a branch of biology dedicated to the study of organisms that live in caves. Like salamanders and bugs and bats. We were here to sample the bat population for any traces of coronavirus."

"Did you find any?"

"No. That's the good news. But Dr. Segal's untimely death is a true tragedy."

"And you maintain it was an accident?"

"What else could it be? We were alone in the third level of Marengo Cave. Nobody else there. Besides, Jon didn't have an enemy in the world. You look up 'nice guy' in the dictionary and you'd see his picture."

"What about that Tidemore woman who discovered the body?"

"As I understand it, she was up in the Crystal Palace, not down on the lower level. Jon probably bumped his head coming out of Blowing Bat Crawl. It's a tight fit. He and I always had trouble getting through. Anybody with a chest size more than 45 inches can't make it."

"Yes, I've seen it, a narrow entry. Easy to bump your head. But wouldn't Dr. Segal have been wearing a helmet. I understand they are required."

"True, but he might have pulled it off as he was exiting. They can get pretty sweaty. The humidity is high inside the cave."

"Thanks for your insights. I appreciate you coming down here to our part of the state to meet with me," said the sheriff. "However, if you don't mind, I'd also like to talk with the other two members of the – whattaya call it? – Chiropteran Survey Team 27."

"That would be Dr. Bartle and Ranger Marston. But I'm afraid you're out of luck. Hugo Marston is on leave. I think I mentioned his wife was having a baby. It was a boy, by the way – Hugo Jr. And Dr. Bartle flew back East. The National Institutes of Health is located in Bethesda, Maryland."

"Well, I guess I can forego talking with them boys. Pending the coroner's report, I think we can wrap this up. Likely you're right, he banged his head on an overhead rock. An accidental death. Finding the body scared that Tidemore woman half to death. She thought she was seeing monsters. Woman's a bit cuckoo, you ask me."

"Okay, if you have no further questions, I'll be heading back to Evanston. It's a good six-hour drive from here."

"Sorry to have taken up so much of your time. But you've been very helpful."

"No problem. I needed to come down anyway. Seems I left my Estwing E3-22P down in Stewart Hall. That's the big cavern on the third level. After I'm finished here with you, I'll drop by the cave to retrieve it."

"Estwing E3-22P – what's that?"

"A geologist's rock hammer. Kind of like a pick axe. We cavers use them for chipping away obstructing rocks on occasion. Not that we ever like to damage any cave formations. But a rock hammer comes in handy now and then."

"So you guys were studying bats?"

"Right. We normally do that to monitor populations and watch out for white-nose syndrome. That's a fungal disease which has resulted in a dramatic decrease of the North American bat population. You can spot it by white patches on a bat's muzzle or wings."

"How do you catch 'em?"

"Mostly we use mist nets – a loose mesh that's practically invisible when strung up between two poles in the dark. Their 'radar' doesn't detect it. Bats get caught in it when they fly by. Then we collect such information as the type of species or weight, check for disease, or band the bat so it can be tracked. Then the bat is released to continue its nightly activities."

"Sounds like a spider catching bugs in its web."

"You get the idea. But we catch and release. We don't eat them."

"I've heard people in some places like China eat them. Wasn't that what caused the Covid-19 virus?"

"No one is quite sure where the virus came from – bats, a scaly anteater called a pangolin, or escaping from a virology lab in Wuhan. At this point it's anybody's guess."

"Then why is the National Institutes of Health having you check our Indiana Bats."

"Just a precaution."

~ ~ ~

Indiana Bats (*Myotis sodalis*) are flying mammals with soft dark-gray fur. They look similar to brown bats and northern long-eared bats. One way that scientists can tell the difference between these species is by the size of their feet and the length of their toe hairs.

They live an average of 5 to 10 years, although some have been known to reach 14 years of age.

The Indiana Bat is both a state and federally protected species. It became listed as endangered in the late '60s due to human disturbance of caves that the bats use for winter hibernating. Indiana Bats are vulnerable because they hibernate in large colonies in very few caves. 85% of the entire known population winters in only seven caves. About 23% of these bats hibernate in caves in Indiana.

They are also susceptible to white-nose syndrome (*Pseudogymnoascus destructans*), a fungus disease that manifests itself as a white growth on the muzzles and wing membranes of affected bats. Apparently, WNS prematurely expends the fat reserves needed for winter survival. Since 2006, the disease has killed an estimated 6.7 million bats in the eastern United States and Canada.

Bats are beneficial to Indiana's ecosystem, in that they eat many night-flying insects and crop pests. One bat can eat between 600 to 1,000 mosquitoes and other flying pests in just one hour. If bats were to disappear, the insect population would boom, causing crop failure, economic damage, and human illness.

Bats are fragile and should not be handled. Also, bats like many wild mammals can carry rabies. But bats are shy animals and generally do not attack humans. Vampire bats are another story, but there are no *Desmodus rotundus* found in Indiana.

Coronaviruses are often detected in bats, cats, and camels. The viruses live in, but do not infect. these animals. They can spread to other species and mutate. Covid-19 spreads from human to human, bats not being a part of the transmission stream. Most people infected with the virus will experience mild to moderate respiratory illness and recover. However, some will become seriously ill or die.

There are more than 1,400 species of bats in the world, with 45 of them in the US, and 13 in Indiana. Bats account for one of every five mammals. There are an estimated one billion bats worldwide.

Based on a 1985 census of hibernating bats, the Indiana Bat population is estimated around 244,000. That's a lot of bats.

Chapter Twenty-Two

The Expedition Begins

Maddy made reservations for the Caving Adventure tour, six tickets in all. Cookie volunteered to drive, so everybody piled into her roomy Range Rover that Saturday morning. The Range Rover Sport offered seating for seven, so there was plenty of room. This $70,900 SE with a P360 3.0 liter engine had been last year's Christmas present from Cookie's husband Ben.

Leaving at 7:30 a.m., they arrived at Marengo Cave at precisely 11:45. Their scheduled appointment was at noon. Traffic was light that weekend. They had made good time.

First thing, they picked up their tickets at the gift shop counter, then followed their guide – Lenny Ray Scroggins again – to get outfitted and receive a rundown of the safety guidelines for deep caving. Each of them was issued a helmet and a headlamp. Having been here before, Maddy knew the routine. They would get to keep the LED lights (Maddy's light from the previous trip was at home, so she got a new one).

"Don't get frightened if we run into other cavers down there," Lenny Ray forewarned. "There's a guy from Northwestern University here today. Looking for something he lost. He's kind of a regular, has the run of the place."

"He's down there alone?" asked Bootsie. She'd just heard the lecture about never caving by yourself.

"No, he's got one of our guides with him, my brother Gary. Ol' Gare's very experienced. He's been doing this eight years, twice as long as me."

"Oh great," N'yen muttered. "We get the inexperienced brother." But he kept his voice low, so only Sissy heard him.

"*Shhhh,*" she nudged him with her elbow.

Lenny Ray led them to the narrow metal door on the Crystal Palace side of the cave. "Follow me," he instructed. "We're going down into the second level. It's well lighted. An easy stroll around the edge of Mirror Lake. From there we will descend to the third level. That will be a little more difficult. Expect to get very muddy."

The group trailed behind their guide, *oo*ing and *ahh*ing at the amazing limestone formations. Maddy had seen them before, but found them just as impressive the second time around. Bootsie was a little nervous, but Lizzie nudged her along.

Within ten minutes, they came to the bronze plaque that announced Blowing Bat Crawl. The entrance looked more like a crack in the rock than the portal to another underground world.

"For this off-the-grid caving experience, we'll be going down to the lowest level. Some of it's going to be crawling on your belly. That's why they call it a 'crawl.' Is everybody okay with that?"

There was a faint muttering of affirmation.

"At the bottom, you will find the largest cavern in the state. The limestone can get pretty slippery in places, so watch your footing and don't fall," he continued. "And please stay together. Like in swimming, we're going to use the buddy system, so pair up."

Maddy took Cookie, Lizzie matched up with Bootsie, and N'yen, of course, chose Sissy. Wisdom would have been to place each of the kids with an adult, but the two youngsters wouldn't hear of it. After all, they were both sixteen – only a few years younger than their guide.

Lenny Ray led the way, lowering himself feet-first into the crevice. Maddy and Cookie followed, eyes on Lenny Ray's bobbing headlamp. Next came the two kids, with Lizzie and Bootsie bringing up the rear.

The beams of their headlamps swept the darkness, like a light saber fight in *Star Wars*. "Easy does it," called the guide. "Don't bump your heads."

"Thank goodness we're wearing helmets," said Bootsie.

That comment made Maddy think of the dead man – Dr. Jonathan Segal – suffering a blow to the top of his head. Why wasn't he wearing his helmet? These hard hats were regulation gear for cavers. Was a helmet found? She didn't remember seeing one near the man's body.

She'd have to follow up on that.

Maybe she could get Chief Jim Purdue to ask Sheriff Barneswell about that helmet. Did he find it? Something just wasn't right about this "accidental death"!

~ ~ ~

Having checked into French Lick Springs the night before, Harry Teague and his new bride had enjoyed a delicious prime rib dinner at the 1875 Steakhouse, then repaired to the casino. Harry lost $212 on the roulette wheel; Penny made $32 on the slots.

They had reserved a suite with a living room. It featured a well-stocked wet bar and a balcony overlooking one of the resort's four golf courses. The Peter Dye Course has been voted the No. 1 course in Indiana for twelve years in a row.

As the brochures say, French Lick Resort offers "Old World opulence amid modern comforts served with Midwestern charm."

Important thing, the beds were comfortable. After all, this was their honeymoon.

The next morning, Harry wanted to go back to the casino and recoup his losses. "I've got a new system I wanna try," he said. "Alternating my bets on red and black. I think that'll improve my odds."

"No, I want to go to Marengo Cave," she countered.

"Where?"

"You know, the cave where Tilly Tidemore found that dead college professor."

"Why there? We can have a nice breakfast – it's included with the room – then hit the casino. You were doing pretty good on the slots last night."

"Thirty bucks is pocket change. But it will pay for a tour of the cave."

"What's to see in a cave?"

"Stalactites, stalagmites."

"Who wants to crawl around in a dirty old cave when we could be wallowing in luxury here at French Lick?"

"Oh, don't be a stick in the mud."

"Being stuck in the mud – that's what I'm trying to avoid."

It was a losing argument.

~ ~ ~

"What was that?" muttered Sissy, waving the beam of her Ray-O-Vac along the cave walls. There was no trail lighting down here on the third level.

"Probably a bat," replied N'yen. "Don't worry. They're harmless."

"Says you. I've seen all them old Christopher Lee *Dracula* movies. Vampires can turn into bats."

"You're *sooo* superstitious, Sissy Jackson. Is everybody from the South crazy like that."

"I am not crazy. I'm cautious."

"Then watch where you step. These rocks are slick as greasy grimy gopher guts."

"Ugh."

Maddy's voice came from ahead of them "Remember why we're down here. We're looking for a bloody rock … or some other blunt instrument. Something that could have been used to kill Professor Segal."

"There's a zillion rocks down here," whined Sissy.

"We're only looking for one," said N'yen.

"Right," Bootsie responded from the rear. "Use your flashlights to search the ground. You won't find it on the walls or ceiling."

"Look for a helmet too," suggested Maddy.

"Why a helmet?" asked Bootsie.

"Just a hunch."

"Darn," grumbled Lizzie in the darkness ahead. "I just broke a nail."

"You're not supposed to touch anything," warned the guide.

"I didn't. I broke it on my stupid flashlight."

Bootsie said, "It's going to be hard to spot a rock used to brain the professor. Everything's brown down here. Like looking at a sepia-toned photograph."

Cookie spoke up. "Many factors impact the shape and color of speleothems, including the chemical composition of the rock and water."

"Speleothems?" said Lizzie.

"Speleothems are formations created over time by mineral deposits accumulating in natural caves. Like those stalactites," she pointed to the cave's ceiling. "The ones comprised of pure calcium carbonate or calcium sulfate are translucent and colorless. The presence of iron oxide or copper produces a reddish brown color. Manganese oxide creates darker colors such as black or dark brown. Speleothems can also be brown due to the presence of mud and silt."

"How do you know all that?" said the guide, impressed.

"Wikipedia," she shrugged off the question.

"Hey, what's this?" said Bootsie, focusing her light on a shiny object to the right of the trail.

"Looks like some kind of tool," noted Lizzie, her gaze following Bootsie's light.

"It's a rock pick," said Maddy,

"Actually, it's an Estwing E3-22P," observed the guide, looking over Bootsie's shoulder.

"What's that?" asked Maddy.

"A geologist's rock hammer," he explained. "I know because it belongs to one of the Northwestern bat researchers. He lost it last trip. He's down here searching for it right now."

"Well, I found it for him," said Bootsie. Proud of her keen eye. "Do you think there's a reward?"

Chapter Twenty-Three

Subterranean Honeymoon

Harry and Penny paid at the counter for tickets to the Crystal Palace Tour. This was the one that would take them past Blowing Bat Crawl, the spot where that professor's body had been found. Harry thought it a tad ghoulish of his wife to want to visit the crime scene, but as a cop he was used to dealing with rubberneckers.

But Penny was a journalist, he reminded himself. A built-in curiosity went with the job. And recently she had been officially given the *Burpyville Gazette*'s crime beat. Along with came a weekly column titled "Crime In Our Time." His wife's career was on a roll.

The couple was assigned to the next tour, a small group of six people. It was scheduled to depart in ten minutes. Clearly a tactic to give people ample time to browse in the 3,000-square-feet gift shop.

Penny bought a geode, not a rock you'd find in this cave, but quite pretty. A spherical rock split in half, its hollow interior displayed purple crystals. It would make a great paperweight.

"Be right back, hon," she said to her husband. "I'm going to put this in the car." They had driven down in her late-model robin's-egg-blue Volkswagen Passant. It got pretty good mileage.

"Don't doddle, Hon. The tour's gonna start in just a few minutes."

She winked. "Wouldn't miss it for the world. I'll hurry."

Penny walked down the path to the parking area, beeped the VW with her key fob, and stuffed the geode into the glove compartment where it couldn't be seen by passersby. As she glanced up, she noticed a dusty green Chevy pickup circling the lot in search of a parking spot. The driver was a handsome man with a rugged cast to his face, a square unshaven jaw that made Penny think of a cowboy or a lumberjack. His dark-green shirt looked like it might be the tunic of a uniform; she could see a round patch sewn onto the sleeve.

She wasn't sure what caught her eye. Maybe it was the intense look on the man's face, the squinted eyes, the firm line of his lips. For some reason, she wondered if he had a gun rack in the back of his cab, but couldn't tell for sure from this angle. She ducked below the dashboard, trying to avoid being spotted. It was an irrational reaction that she couldn't begin to explain.

Well, then again, maybe she could.

It came back to her exactly whom he reminded her of. That was a flash from her past. No need to go there!

Nonetheless, Penny kept her head down. She heard the pickup come to a stop, the engine switch off, the bang of the driver's side door as the man climbed out slamming it shut. She could hear his boots crunching on the gravel as he walked up the hill toward the wood-framed gift shop.

Penny counted to ten, then followed him. As stealthy as a cat, she trailed thirty paces behind. His presence was like an ice cube sliding along her spine.

~ ~ ~

It was driving Aggie nuts that she couldn't be with the Quilters Club for the expedition into the belly of Marengo Cave. But she was stuck at school. She hated being left out of a big case – especially one involving her mother. Aggie loved her mom dearly, but worried for her well-being. She had witnessed Tilly Tidemore's gradual deterioration, slipping inch-by-inch into a fantasy world in which she barely recognized her husband or kids.

Her mom imagined herself as a princess and her husband as a handsome prince. After all, they lived in a "castle," didn't they? Aggie was seen as a young warrior, somewhere between Joan of Arc and a teenage Wonder Woman. Aggie's sisters were pixies – although Aggie would have cast them as the three witches from *Macbeth*. Tilly saw her father and mother as a version of King Arthur and Guinevere without a Lancelot. N'yen was Puck personified, stepping full-blown from the pages of *A Midsummer Night's Dream*, while Aunts Hilda and Helga seemed to be those dotty old ladies from the movie *Arsenic and Old Lace*. Marybelle Olsen was perfect as Mary Poppins (a fantasy Aggie shared), and Cookie and Ben Bentley were like major characters from *The Lord of the Rings*. Chief Jim Purdue was viewed as an embodiment of Gary Cooper in *High Noon*, which was strange in that Jim was chubby and bald, nothing like the lanky, laconic actor with wavy hair under that cowboy hat. Lizzie and her husband Edgar could have been a redheaded Beauty and a shaggy-haired Beast.

None of it real.

That cursed Crackleton blood, Aggie told herself. Wondering if it coursed through her own veins like a raging River of No Return. Would she someday slip into madness herself?

Aggie tried to reach her cousin N'yen on his iPhone, but no answer. He was probably already deep inside that cave, no cell signal available within its limestone depths.

Drat!

Chapter Twenty-Four

The Park Ranger

When Penny walked into the gift shop, she was taken aback to see the strange man talking with her husband. What was there about the guy that made the hairs on her arm stand up like tiny bristles? Oh yeah, that!

"Hi, sweetie," Harry greeted her. "Look who I bumped into – Hugo Marston. Hugo's a ranger with the Department of Natural Resources. We worked together on that missing person case in the Hoosier National Forest a few years back."

"That one turned out okay," the ranger nodded. "Found the guy trapped under a fallen tree. Just a broken leg and a little worse for the wear from exposure to the elements. As it turned out, he was an illegal logger. So after we saved his sorry butt, he got two years in the FCI."

"FCI?" repeated Penny, trying to follow the conversation.

"The Federal Correctional Institution at Terre Haute," translated her husband. New to the crime beat at the *Burpyville Gazette*, she wasn't used to all the cop talk. But she was a quick learner.

"Are you going caving?" she asked the ranger. Making polite conversation by stating the obvious.

"Guess you could say that," confirmed Harry. "He's in our tour group."

"Actually, I've been working this cave as part of the Chiropteran Survey Team 27. That's a research project with the NIH. Today I came back to look for something I left in the cave, but there's not a guide available to go in with me. So I'll tag along with the Crystal Palace Tour, then climb down the crawlspace to the lower level."

"There's a lower level?"

"Technically, three levels. The lower level was discovered about thirty years ago when explorers broke through a fissure, revealing an unknown crawlspace. It led them down to a stream level that contained the largest room of any cave in Indiana. This discovery added 3 ½ miles to the cave's length, making it about 5 miles in all – one of the longest caves in the entire state."

"Wow. Can we go down there with you?"

" 'Fraid not. That's one of their Cave Exploring packages. You're on one of the Walking Tours."

"The third level isn't a walking tour?"

Ranger Marston laughed. "It's more of a crawling-through-the-mud-on-your-belly tour."

"But you're going down there."

"Just a quick side trip. Remember I'm a state park ranger. Gives me certain privileges."

"It would be so cool to see an underground stream."

"You'll see a pool on the Crystal Palace Tour. Mirror Lake, it's very pretty."

"But this is our honeymoon. Couldn't you make it memorable for us by taking us with you to the lower level? Like you said, you have special privileges as a park ranger.

"Sorry. Harry understands. I might get suspended if I broke the rules."

"Spoilsport," said Penny. But she made it sound as if she were joking.

"You'll enjoy your tour. Marengo is considered the most highly decorated cavern in the Interior Lowlands of the US. And the Crystal Palace is beautiful, a wonderland of sorts."

"But I wanted to see where that murder took place."

"Uh, what do you know about that?"

Harry spoke up. "My wife is a reporter for the *Burpyville Gazette*. She has her ear to the ground – so to speak."

"Oh, a reporter. Well, first of all, they just ruled it an accidental death, not a murder. And it didn't occur in the lower level. It happened at the entrance of Blowing Bat Crawl. You will pass it on the Crystal Palace Tour. That's where Dr. Segal died."

"Lucky us, we signed up for the right tour," trilled Penny.

Harry got that cop look on his face, as if he were fitting clues together. "Say, Hugo, wasn't that dead guy a member of the bat project you're working on?"

"Matter of fact, he was. I was with him that day. We were a four-man team. But nobody saw it happen; we'd already finished our work for the day. Guess ol' Jon got careless, bumped his head climbing outta the hole."

"A tragedy," muttered Penny. The polite thing to say. But she was wondering how an experienced caver like Hugo's partner could "bump his head" hard enough to kill himself.

~ ~ ~

Down below, Dr. Jason Wiener was climbing over boulders in the passage above the waterfall, moving toward the far end of the stream. He was looking for his rock hammer.

He was very fond of the Estwing E3-22P, especially the comfort of its molded shock reduction grip which reduced vibrations caused by impact. At 13 inches long, the 22-ounce pointed-tip hammer featured a fully polished head. What's more, its head and handle were forged as one piece.

He last remembered using it in Stewart Hall on the lower level. Approximately 350 feet wide and over 250 feet long with a ceiling height of 60 feet, Stewart Hall is the largest cavern in any Indiana caves. That rock hammer could be anywhere in that massive room, or worse dropped somewhere in the mountain of breakdown that leads into the Hall. To be thorough, Jason Wiener decided to start above the waterfall and work his way back toward the exit.

His guide – Gary Scroggins – carried a $150 Olight M30 flashlight that could last 90 minutes at 700 lumens on 4 x 130. "When you absolutely, positively have to light up every last corner of a giant cavern, accept no substitutes," Gary liked to say.

Wiener's own flashlight was Fenix TK40, pretty floody at 630 lumens. Together, they added illumination to the darkened cave. Unlike the tour trails above them, the lower level was unlighted. As dark as midnight without their headlamps and flashlights.

"You sure you left it this far back?" grumbled the guide. He had tours to conduct for paying customers. Accommodating the Chiropteran Survey Team 27 was more like a courtesy, no compensation involved. But Gary's boss liked to assist the NIH project in a show of ecological good faith.

"I'm not sure. Let's move more toward the waterfall."

"Gee, it's only a $30 geologist's hammer. I'll buy you one, if you'll call off this search and let me get back to work."

"I'm rather fond of this one. My wife gave it to me on my birthday six years ago. I'd turned 40, a milestone."

"The way you're carrying on about that stupid hammer, you'd think it was what bopped Professor Segal on the head or something."

"Don't say that. If somebody heard you, they might think you're serious."

"Who's gonna hear me down here. We're alone – just you, me, and several thousand bats."

Jason Wiener focused his TK40 light on the guide. "Keep up that crazy kinda talk and when I find my hammer I'm definitely going to hit you on the head with it."

"C'mon, I was just kidding."

Chapter Twenty-Five

Last of the Quads

Aunt Hilda and Aunt Helga did not get the chance for a natural passing. That very morning, their Rolls Royce Silver Cloud was hit head-on by a semi carrying cement blocks. Doc Medford said their deaths were likely instantaneous. Aunt Hilda had been driving, not looking as she turned onto Burpyville Highway. She had been talking with her sister about what a miracle it was that Tilly was nearly back to normal. As usual, her eyes were not on the road.

The good news – if there can be such a thing with a tragic event like this – was that they had signed all the papers last night to turn over their fortune to their family. Barnabus Soltairé had come by the Mansion with all the necessary documents. Maddy and Maisie had served as witnesses. Barney, who always thought of everything, had brought a notary along with him.

Maddy didn't get word of the fatality right away, in that she and her friends were 200 feet down inside the largest cavern in the state, no cell phone signal able to penetrate the thick limestone barrier.

Beau and his sister-in-law Maisie went over to Yost & Yost Funeral Home to identify the bodies. Despite the horrendous collision – the Rolls was a twisted ball of metal – the two women were unblemished, looking as if merely taking an afternoon nap.

The driver of the semi had been killed too. He was an ex-Marine who had escaped a series of IEDs – roadside bombs – while serving in Afghanistan, only to die at the hands of two little old ladies in Indiana. The insurance would have paid off handsomely, but he had no living relatives to make a claim. The lonely life of a long-distance trucker was like a therapy for his PTSD, an affliction he'd brought back from the War.

~ ~ ~

Doc Medford saw no point in telling anyone of his cancer diagnosis for Hilda Hoople. God had taken care of the situation, sparing her from uncomfortable chemotherapy and a painful death. At least that was his opinion. He attended Peaceful Meadows, the Baptist church on the other side of the Town Square. The one with the tall spire, as if reaching toward Heaven. He was a very religious man for a coroner.

Maybe God knew what he was doing with Helga also. She had disappeared for years, letting people think she had drowned in Gruesome Gorge State Park. Turns out, she had been living in solitude up on Boyd Aitkens' watermelon land. Her brief resurrection had given her the opportunity to really say goodbye to her family and friends, Doc told himself.

Doc Medford had no opinion on the trucker, but his life had seemed sad and empty. Maybe God had something to say about that too.

Being both a medical man and the town's part-time coroner, Franklin Medford saw a lot of death. He relied on his faith to see him through all the sadness that accompanied his job. He'd become a doctor to save lives; now he more often seemed to be watching lives end. Oh well, it was in the Lord's hands.

Doc Medford never missed a Sunday sermon at Peaceful Meadows. He was a deacon in the church. He and Old Tom Dancy were tasked with passing the collection plates.

Too bad about the loss of the Hoople sisters. They didn't make it to church every Sunday, but when they showed up their tithing was very generous. Their passing would be a financial loss for Peaceful Meadows.

Chapter Twenty-Six

The Confrontation

Maddy and her Quilters Club friends were still poking around the stalactite-filled chamber when Bootsie spotted the Estwing rock hammer laying there in the muck as if it had tumbled down the slope from the narrow crawlspace.

As Bootsie reached down to pick it up, a voice stopped her short. "Don't touch that rock pick," ordered someone standing nearby in the darkness. Sounded like the voice was coming from the crevice that linked the Crystal Palace with this lower level.

"Say, who's there?" shouted Lenny Ray Scroggins. He pointed his flashlight beam in that direction, but it didn't pick out anyone. "Is that you, Dr. Wiener?"

No response.

"Gary, are you there?" he tried again, calling to his brother.

A figure stepped into their lights. A man, judging by his bulk. Reaching up to his helmet, he snapped on his twin headlamps, the beams illuminating his craggy face. "No, it's just me, Hugo Marston."

"Oh, Ranger Marston. What are you doing down here? Are you with Dr. Wiener and Gary?"

"Came down to join them. I thought I'd help them look for Jason's rock hammer. He seemed awfully upset over losing it."

"You're not supposed to be down here alone. But I suppose it's all right if you're hooking up with Dr. Wiener and my brother."

"Yeah, that's the plan."

"We haven't seen 'em. Maybe they came out before we got here."

"Or maybe they're farther back in the cave. It goes on for – what? – three more miles."

"Uh-huh. Could be they're up there past the falls. They'll be happy to know Mrs. Purdue just found the missing hammer. She's got mighty sharp eyes."

"Yeah, Jason will be pleased."

"Hold on, I'll get the hammer for you," volunteered Bootsie. Taking a step forward, her hand extended toward the rock hammer.

"No, stop! You might smear the fingerprints."

"W-what?"

"Fingerprints?" said Lenny Ray. "Whatcha talkin' about, Mr. Marston."

The light of his twin headlamps gave the ranger a sinister look, like when kids shine their flashlight beam at an angle on their face to play monster. "This might be the blunt object that killed Jon Segal," he said "That would make it evidence. We shouldn't touch it."

"But the sheriff has declared Dr. Segal's death an accident," replied Lenny Ray. "Said he banged his head on a rock."

"I still have a suspicion that it could've been foul play. That's why I came down here looking for Jason Wiener's missing rock hammer. Seems too coincidental that his hammer went missing at the same time Jon got killed by a blunt instrument."

Maddy was thinking the same thing. But was Hugo Marston the good citizen he pretended to be? Or did he have his own agenda?

"Hold on there," echoed a voice from behind them, in the direction of the waterfall. "I heard that. What are you saying, Hugo? That I killed Jon Segal?"

The Quilters Club turned to see Dr. Jason Wiener emerge from the darkness on the other side of the stream, his guide in tow. He looked angry, his face bathed in light from the cyclopean headlamp affixed to his helmet.

"Jason, there you are," blurted the ranger, surprised by the professor's sudden appearance. "I came down here looking for you."

"I heard you just tell them you were looking for my hammer."

"That too."

"What's this malarkey about fingerprints? Of course my prints are on the Estwing. After all, it's *my* rock hammer."

"That's right," Maddy followed the logic. "Finding Dr. Wiener's fingerprint on the hammer wouldn't prove anything. You'd expect them to be there. But if *your* fingerprints are on it, that would prove something else."

"Hey, are you accusing me of clobbering that pretentious Lothario?" responded the ranger. "My prints wouldn't be on there in any case. I always wear gloves when I'm caving." He held up a hand in front of his light to prove the point.

"Not that day," countered Dr. Wiener. "You said you left your gloves in your truck and didn't want to go back for them."

Hugo Marston took a step forward. "Who you gonna believe – some flighty college professor or me, a park ranger?

I'm a law enforcement officer, after all. What motive would I have for killing Jon Segal?"

Maddy said, "You just referred to him as a Lothario. What did you mean by that?"

"Uh, he had a reputation for hitting on his students."

"That's not true," countered Dr. Wiener. "Jon had an impeccable reputation with his kids. It was faculty wives who interested him."

"Not just faculty," growled Hugo Marston. "For him any wife would do."

"You mean like your wife?" responded Maddy.

"Leave Trudy out of this!" shouted the ranger. Suddenly angry. Face contorted in the light of the headlamps.

"His wife just had a baby," said Jason Wiener, sounding contrite.

Sissy Jackson spoke up: "Yeah, but is the baby his'n?" The girl sometimes had no filters. If she thought it, she said it.

"Why you little –" shouted the ranger, taking a step toward the girl.

However, before he could reach her, a shadow leaped from the darkness of the crawlspace, tackling Hugo Marston. The two figures tumbled onto the muddy cavern floor, fists swinging, headlamps casting their beams wildly on the ceiling. Grunts were heard as blows landed. Flashlights rolled aside, coming to a stop as they clinked against stalagmites. Swear words emanated from the struggling combatants.

Hugo Marston managed to disengage himself and scurry aside. Holding up his palms in surrender, he shouted, "Enough, enough."

Harry Teague shakily stood, his meaty hands still balled into fists. "What's this all about?" he asked Bootsie. After all, she was his boss's wife.

"I'm not sure," she admitted, confused by the events that had just transpired. "Something about fingerprints on that rock hammer over there," she pointed.

Maddy stepped in. "Simple – Hugo Marston murdered Dr. Segal in a fit of jealousy over his wife. I expect a DNA test will prove that Ranger Marston's new baby – Hugo Jr. – is actually the child of the late Jonathan Segal."

"That sounds about right to me," said Jason Wiener. "Jon was a womanizer. And I've heard rumors about him and Hugo's wife."

"So he used your hammer to kill Dr. Segal?"

"Looks like it. I lost my rock hammer the other day when we were down here in the cave. Apparently, Hugo found it and used it to clock Jon in the head."

"That's a lie. It's true Segal had been seeing my wife, but I didn't kill him."

"Says you," replied Sissy.

"Yeah, you sure look guilty," nodded N'yen. Supportive of his girlfriend.

Bootsie agreed. "As my husband Jim would say, you had the Means (the hammer), the Motive (your wife), and the Opportunity (alone with him in a dark cave)."

"I never had the hammer. I came back to help Jason look for it – only to have him turn on me, the jerk!"

"Hey, who you calling a jerk, you murderer?"

"I tell you, I didn't do it."

"One of you guides go topside and phone the sheriff," interrupted Harry Teague. "Let him sort this out."

"Good idea," nodded Maddy, her silver hair bobbing in the faint light. "You go, Lenny. Your brother can stay here with us."

"Sure thing," the boy agreed. Happy to get away from these crazy people.

"Harry Teague," said Bootsie, "how did you magically show up just in the nick of time? Marengo is a little out of your normal jurisdiction."

"I'm down here on my honeymoon. Penny wanted to see the cave. When we bumped into Hugo here, she got suspicious. So when he split off from the tour group, she insisted I follow him down Blowing Bat Crawl to see what he was up to. Good thing I did, looks like."

"You came down the crawlspace without him hearing you trailing behind?" said N'yen, impressed with the lawman's stealth. "You're a regular Ninja."

"Wasn't easy. I turned my lights off, so I had to come down in the dark. Hard to do that without making a sound. Practically broke my leg on them rocks. Surprised he didn't hear me bumping and thumping, crawling along behind him with just the glow of his headlamps to guide me."

~ ~ ~

Sheriff Jake Barneswell personally came out to the cave to take charge of the prisoner. He was feeling pretty embarrassed at declaring Dr. Segal's death an accident. Perhaps he had jumped the gun.

"This is a little awkward," Barneswell admitted. "A county sheriff and an off-duty police deputy arresting a state park ranger."

"Hugo's not a bad guy," said Dr. Wiener. "Jon Segal simply pushed him too far, not only having a fling with his wife, but also impregnating her. I'd have probably killed him too, if he'd done that to me."

Sheriff Barneswell rubbed his chin. "Maybe a good lawyer can get him off on the grounds that it was a crime of passion, that he simply lost control of his reasoning when he discovered his wife's new baby wasn't his."

"That's right. He could argue that it wasn't premeditated," suggested Harry. "After all, he didn't bring a gun or other weapon – merely used a pick ax that he found on the cave floor."

"Gentlemen," admonished Maddy, "you are the arresting officers. Not the counsel for the defense."

"Hey, stay out of this, lady," grumbled Hugo Marston. "They're giving me some good advice."

Maddy raised her chin in defiance. "You committed a murder and were willing to let my daughter take the blame for it. Don't look to me for sympathy."

"I tell you, I didn't do it," he replied.

Chapter Twenty-Seven

Tragedy x Two

Beau reached Maddy just as she was finishing up with Sheriff Barneswell. The sheriff had taken statements from each member of the Quilters Club (except for underaged N'yen and Sissy). All the stories matched with Harry's. And his matched with Dr. Wiener's and the two guides.

"Pooh Bear, I think we caught the killer," said Maddy. "It was a park ranger. Tilly's name is cleared." She caught her breath. "Why are you calling? Do you miss me?"

"I've got terrible news," Beau said. Then told her about Aunt Hilda and Aunt Helga.

Maddy was stunned.

Sure, the two women had been octogenarians, but everyone had expected them to live forever. They were (as Marybelle Olsen used to say) "fit as a butcher's dog." Maddy would have said "healthy as a horse." Doc Medford might have had a different opinion.

"Come home as soon as you can. The family is gathering at the Mansion. Maisie and Freddie's brood are already here. Bill and Kathy are on their way down from Chicago. Aggie has booked a fight into Indianapolis. She'll ride down to Caruthers Corners with Barney Solitairé."

"We're heading home right now. Thank goodness, they died instantly. No pain, no suffering."

"Drive carefully," Beau said.

"Wish I'd said that to Aunt Hilda and Aunt Helga," sniffled Maddy. Fighting back the tears, but it was a losing battle.

Chapter Twenty-Eight
Headliner

Penny got the scoop. The *Burpyville Gazette*'s front page heralded:

Gazette Reporter Fingers Cave Killer
Exclusive by Penny Heath

Sheriff Jake Barneswell had asked her, "What made you suspicious of Hugo Marston in the first place?"

Penny shrugged sheepishly. "He reminded me of my first husband."

"You were married before?" blurted Harry Teague. A look of astonishment on his face. This was obviously news to him.

"Just for about fifteen minutes. It didn't work out."

"Don't you think you should've mentioned this detail about your past to me?" said Harry.

"Would it have made any difference? You'd still have married me, wouldn't you?"

"Yeah, but I had a right to know."

"Now you do. I didn't think it was important."

"Mind sharing his name?"

"Like I said, it's not important. But since you ask, it was Terry McGonagall."

"The son of former Burpyville mayor Sean McGonagall?"

"He was a jerk."

"Son or father?"

"Both."

"Was your marriage to Terry the reason you went after Mayor McGonagall, accusing him of being a crime figure on the front page of the newspaper?"

"Maybe a teeny little bit. Terry is the one who dropped a hint that his old man wasn't on the up and up."

"You almost got fired."

"The paper had liability insurance. Mayor McGonagall got $20,000 to sooth his injured feelings."

~ ~ ~

Hugo Marston was transferred to Indy. The tiny jail in Marengo was only suited to accommodate the occasional overnight drunk. Beside, this was a murder case. Marengo didn't have a district attorney or prosecutor. Or even a courthouse.

Although it was circumstantial evidence – and Marston kept denying his guilt – he was charged with first-degree murder in the death of Dr. Jonathan Livingston Segal. The lawyer he hired was trying to get him to do a deal and claim it was a crime of passion, but Marston wouldn't hear of it. He fired the lawyer and accepted a public defender.

The Indiana Department of Natural Resources put him on suspension till the matter could be resolved one way or the other.

When his wife Trudy came to visit him at the Marion County Jail, he had one message for her: "Call your brother."

Chapter Twenty-Nine
A Change of Direction

The funeral was somber. Midwesterners see death as a low-key affair, no parades or bands as in New Orleans, no lavish Irish Wakes like you find in Boston. Pleasant Glades Cemetery reflects the midwestern values of strong work ethic, modesty, and being unremarkable. The markers are neat, tidy, and all nearly identical. Nothing flashy, no "Look Homeward, Angel" monuments, no mausoleums …

… until you go down the hill to the Old Section, that all-but-abandoned dell where broken-down mausoleums and crypts form a village of the dead. Founding Fathers and early settlers are buried here. Along with the most prominent of citizens.

Hilda and Helga Hoople, formerly the richest people in the town, qualified for interment in the Old Section of Pleasant Glades. A sizeable crowd had gathered for the burial service. After all the Caruthers Corners Restoration Coalition that rebuilt the town after the 2018 Northeast Indiana Tornado had been funded by Hilda and Helga. A lot of people enjoyed new homes thanks to them.

Maddy and her family were dressed in black. She was surrounded by her friends – Lizzie, Cookie, and Bootsie – offering solace. Off to the side stood Beau and their husbands.

N'yen and Aggie were there on compassionate leaves from their respective universities. Sissy got to stand with the family.

Needless to say, Maddy was taking Hilda and Helga's deaths hard. "Maybe they wouldn't have been driving around if I'd been there to look after them," she confided to her friends. "Instead, we were off crawling through mud in that stupid cave."

"Don't be silly," said Cookie, the more reasonable of the group. "Those two old gals were driving about all the time, whether you were here or not."

"That's right," echoed Lizzie. "They've been driving themselves about ever since the chauffeur left. That was twenty-some years ago."

"But neither of them had driver's licenses ..."

"Yes, Jim had several talks with them about that, but they didn't take," said the police chief's wife. "He even threatened to impound their car."

"But you go gently with the town's biggest benefactors," added Cookie by way of explanation.

"I know, I know," moaned Maddy. "But I ... I ... I just can't believe they're gone."

~ ~ ~

Oscar Beanie, caretaker of Pleasant Glade and town drunk, watched as the funeral party faded away from the gravesite. The Hoople Mausoleum was almost as impressive as the Hoople Mansion that overlooked the town, its marble façade better upkept than the surrounding structures. Being that this section of the cemetery housed early settlers and Town Founders, it wasn't used much anymore and had been let go. Other than mowing the grass, the caretaker rarely came down here to the Old Section.

Barnabas Solitairé was among the stragglers, holding back for a final goodbye. Having been raised in the Mansion, the Quadruplets were like family to him. Managing their Foundation had been a privilege, even after his lucrative years as a mob lawyer. He was going to miss those daffy ol' gals.

Maddy lingered also. Even though she had discovered her relation to the Hooples late in life, she'd come to adore them. Their generosity knew no bounds. She owed so much to them.

"Looks like I'm out of a job," Barney Solitairé said jokingly to Maddy. Referring to the recent dissolution of the Foundation, the fortune divvied among all the members of the extended family.

"Don't cry poor mouth to me," she laughed . "You were already rich from your earlier law practice" – she politely avoided mentioning Sal the Whisperer and Barney's other shady clients – "and Hilda and Helga gave you a generous slice of the Foundation's monies."

"True. I hope that was all right with you and Maisie."

"You deserve a share as much as we did. You have a long history with the Hooples."

"All my life," he nodded.

"And contrary to being out of a job, Maisie and I would like you to continue administrating our funds. Some of my children feel that way too. We had a family meeting. You probably should have been invited."

"That wasn't necessary. I'm still the son of the maid."

"And Maisie and I are Herbie's secret love children. Big deal."

"Sure, Maddy. I'd be happy to help manage the estate, even if it is divided up. I've retired from my law practice and have nothing better to do."

"Thank you, Barney."

"So what do you want me to do?"

"Sell the Mansion."

~ ~ ~

"You're selling the Hoople Mansion?" gasped Cookie when she told them. This was at the regular Tuesday meeting of the Quilters Club. They had almost finished their Crazy Quilts and were talking about what project to do next when Maddy blurted out her plan.

"Yes, for $1."

"That's crazy," said Lizzie, the most money conscious member among them. As the largest stockholder, she practically owned the local Savings & Loan. "The Mansion is worth millions."

"Who's the lucky buyer?" asked Bootsie.

"The town."

"Caruthers Corners?"

"Yes, on the condition they convert it into a low-cost retirement home – one wing for the needy, the second wing for the infirm, and the third devoted to memory care."

"Memory care? You mean like Alzheimer's?" said Lizzie.

"Exactly. There seems to be more of that going round. I don't know if it's something in the drinking water ... or if we're just living longer and letting dementia catch up with us ... but I've read that the disease is increasing. "

Cookie drew on her trick memory. "In Indiana, the number of people over 65 with Alzheimer's is projected to rise by 18.2% from 2020 to 2025 – to 130,000."

"Some people say Granny Crackleton is showing signs," Bootsie interjected.

"How could you tell?" retorted Lizzie. "That old crone's always been demented." She paused, then added, "Sorry, Maddy."

"No offense taken, even if she *is* my biological grandmother."

"About the Mansion," Cookie stirred the conversation back on track. "What will you and your family do? Live on the street?"

"No, silly. My Trust fund is going to buy a house for me and Beau, as well as one for each of our children. Better they live a normal life than wind up in that big stone mausoleum. I've never been comfortable living in that big ostentatious house up there on a hill overlooking the town."

"Maddy, I thought you loved the Hoople Mansion," said Bootsie. Living in the Mansion was akin to occupying a fairytale castle in Bootsie's mind. She had grown up poor ... well poorer than her three friends.

"I do. But I think it could be put to a better use. And that me and my family should get our feet back down to earth. Normal people don't live in a 52-room fortress that would be fit for a medieval king."

"They would if they could," argued Bootsie.

"I don't want to appear to be a feudal ruler looking down from my castle at the serfs below. I want a real house with a kitchen without cooks, a place where I do the housekeeping myself."

"What about Marybelle Olsen?" said Cookie. "You'd put her out of work?"

"No, I'd appoint her director of Hoople Assisted Living LLC. Barney Solitairé is drawing up the papers as we speak."

"Well, this is a big change," sighed Lizzie.

"Change is good," said Maddy.

Chapter Thirty

An Ironclad Alibi

Chief Jim Purdue rang the bell at the Hoople Mansion late that night. Marybelle ushered him into the study and offered him tea or coffee – both of which he turned down – so she went off to fetch Maddy.

Official business, he'd said. That sounded ominous.

Maddy rushed into the room, Beau a few steps behind her. "Jim, what brings you out this time of night," she greeted her visitor. It was nearly 11 p.m. according to the big grandfather clock in the foyer. "Not more bad news, I hope?" The loss of her aunts had shaken her.

"I'm not sure," the police chief admitted. "There are new developments in the Jonathan Segal murder."

"New developments? I thought the case was closed with that ranger's arrest."

"Apparently not. Sheriff Barneswell phoned me to say it's open again. Seems that Dr. Benjamin Bartle, the fourth member of that bat survey team, came forward to give Hugo Marston an alibi. Said he was with him every second as they came out of the cave, that Hugo didn't have any opportunity to bash Dr. Segal on the head. Said Hugo gave him a ride from Marengo to Evanston and then to O'Hare Airport."

Maddy gasped at the news. "You're saying Hugo Marston is innocent?"

"Sure looks that way."

"But if Marston didn't do it, who did?"

"That question's back open. And Tilly's back on the list of Persons of Interest. Thought you'd wanna know. I've already told Mark. He was working late at the Town Hall."

"This means the Quilters Club fingered an innocent man."

"I've been trying to tell you gals to –" But he cut off his words. Now wasn't the time for I-told-you-so's.

~ ~ ~

"My mom needs our help," said Aggie, knocking on N'yen's door at midnight. Still home from college, she'd overheard Chief Purdue's conversation with her Grammy and Grampy. Not that she meant to be eavesdropping, but she'd been on her way to the kitchen for a glass of milk and some watermelon cookies. It'd been hard to find watermelon cookies at bake shops in New Haven, the Connecticut town where Yale University is located.

"Jeez, do you know what time it is?" mumbled her cousin, rubbing the sleep out of his eyes. "I was having a dream about me and Sissy."

"I don't want to hear about your wet dreams."

"Hey, it was about when she and I were down in Marengo Cave. She was lost and I was trying to find her – in the dream, that is."

"That's what I want to talk with you about, going back to the cave to look for more evidence, something that will clear my mom."

"Back to the cave?"

"Well, it would be the first time for me."

"Why do we need to 'clear your mom'? She was cleared when the sheriff arrested that park ranger."

Aggie recounted what she'd overheard. "Turns out, Hugo Marston has an ironclad alibi. So my mom's back to being a suspect."

"So you want to look for evidence to clear her name?"

"That's right."

N'yen wrinkled his brow. "Exactly what kind of evidence would that be?"

Aggie frowned. "Any kind of evidence. We don't have to fill out a search warrant to go to the cave. Just buy a ticket."

"What makes you think there's any evidence to find? We looked the place over pretty good, so did the sheriff's deputies."

"Searching a dark hole with flashlights is not what I'd call looking the place over pretty good. You were lucky to have found your way in and out."

N'yen huffed, "There's only one way in and out, by crawling on your stomach down a hole. And there are bats down there. You may not want to try that."

"If you and Sissy Jackson can do it, so can I. Bats or no bats."

"Go to bed. We'll talk about this in the morning."

"Why can't we go down there right now. I've got my driver's license. We could borrow my mom's crystal-mobile?"

"It's a three-hour drive. And we need a plan. We can talk at breakfast. Sissy's coming over."

"Uncle Jim says they didn't find any blood on that geologist's hammer, so the murder weapon must be something else. Like a rock maybe."

"How would we recognize the murder weapon? One rock looks pretty much like another."

"Can't we take a black light and shine it around? Doesn't that make blood glow in the dark?"

N'yen sighed. "Contrary to popular crime TV shows, blood does not magically appear when you turn on a UV light. Blood absorbs ultraviolet light and will appear black. You need to spray an area with a special chemical additive like luminol for blood to fluoresce."

"I know you've got black lights. You shine them on your posters. Like a sixties hippie. Don't you have any of this luminol stuff?"

"Not a drop. Besides, you can't be spraying that stuff all over the cave walls. It might damage the stalactites, for all I know."

"Hey, you're the science guy."

"Right, just call me Bill Nye Jr."

"There has to be some way we can check for blood traces in the cave."

"Even if there were, I doubt the cave owners would agree to let us do it. It's privately owned, y'know."

"Nothing sneaky we can do?"

"Hmm, maybe one thing …."

"What one thing?" squeaked Aggie.

"Use a dog."

"You mean like a bloodhound?"

"Kinda. In recent years, several law enforcement agencies in Europe and Australia have introduced blood-detection dogs, which are trained to sniff out blood evidence at a crime scene."

"Where would we get a dog like that? My little pooch Tige would have no clue how to sniff out blood. He can barely find his food bowl. Ever since I've been off to college, Marybelle has practically turned him into a lap dog!"

"Not just any dog can do it. It takes one that's specially trained to detect that specific scent."

"Be realistic," she rolled her eyes. "We'll never get our hands on a canine like that."

"*Au contraire, mademoiselle,*" he showed off his French. "I know where to find one."

"Do tell," she said. He now had her complete attention.

N'yen paused to enjoy the fact that he knew something she didn't. "Uncle Jim recently adopted a retired K-9 dog, a German Shepherd that was trained for scent detection with the Chicago Police Department. According to Uncle Jim, the dog's specialty was blood."

"Get out!"

"Honest to goodness. But the trick will be getting Uncle Jim to let us borrow his new pet ... and getting it into the cave. When Grammy and I were there before, the guide said small dogs are allowed inside the cave if they're carried the during the entire tour."

"So?"

"Have you ever seen Uncle Jim's dog? Mörder must weigh a good 80 pounds. No way we can carry that oversized monster. He'd be like a sack of wiggling cement."

"You go borrow – what's his name Mörder? – and I'll figure out how to get him inside the cave."

"Good luck with that."

"Not luck, *mon petit* Einstein. Brains!"

Chapter Thirty-One

The Unexpected Chauffeur

"**H**ere's the deal," said Aggie Tidemore. Her radiant 18-year-old face tried to look contrite. "My Mom is coming with us."

"No way."

"Way."

"Are you sure that's a good idea?" responded N'yen. He didn't want to point out that her mother lived in a world of goblins, demons, and Morlocks.

"I think things are better. The Great Wizardini is a miracle worker."

"Do you think her chemical imbalances can be cured by hypnotism."

"I don't know. But she certainly seems normal ... for the time being. I'll take that. I want my Mom back."

"Okay, your mother's coming along. But for what purpose?"

"Because she wants to confront the place she saw the Morlock kill the professor. Confrontation therapy, she calls it. Besides, that's the only way she'll let us use her car."

"Alright, if *you* do the driving. I trust you behind the wheel of the crystal-mobile more than your mother. She brakes for fairies."

"Be nice. We also have a plan. Mom has rented a cabin at Marengo Cave. They rent cabins. There are four of them there."

"Can we all fit into one tiny cabin?"

"I don't think that will be a problem. We got Cabin 3. It sleeps up to eight people. There will only be four of us – plus the dog. Plenty of room."

"Have you figured out how we're going to get into that cave with a dog?"

"Maybe. But do you have the dog?"

He nodded. "Uncle Jim was skeptical, but with Aunt Bootsie's urging he said we could borrow his dog overnight. Being a former K-9 dog, Mörder's well-trained."

"What does Mörder mean anyway?"

"It's German for Murderer, but Uncle Jim says to pay no attention to the name. He's gentle as a puppy."

"Let's hope so. I don't want to get on the bad side of an 80-pound German Shepherd named Murderer."

~ ~ ~

Buck Jackson gave permission for his granddaughter to go on this overnighter with his old pal Beau's daughter, Tilly. Word was she was doing much better these days, no longer the unpredictable daydreamer she'd once been. He had some misgivings but supposed it would be all right as long as Aggie was along. That young lady was eighteen now and in college – so she would keep things on the straight and narrow. She'd always had a level head on her shoulders.

Cecelia's boyfriend – that young Vietnamese who was already in college despite being only 16 – would be along too. People said he was a smart kid, a genius in fact. He knew that the boy would look after Cecelia no matter what.

Now wasn't that a change of the times? Back in the '60s he'd been over there in the jungles shooting at gooks. Now his granddaughter might end up marrying one. So be it.

"What's this trip all about?" he asked Sissy as she packed an overnight bag.

"I'm going caving again," she explained. "Like I did a week or two ago with the Quilters Club."

"But you were with four grown women."

"Aggie's mom will be along."

"Like she's a grown woman? I've heard lots of stories."

"We'll be fine. Besides Aggie will be there. And she's almost grown."

Buck Jackson produced a shiny silver coin. "Here's a dime. You should always carry one, case you need t' phone home for help."

"Thanks, Gramps. But pay phones are a thing of the past. Haven't you noticed there aren't any phone booths anymore?"

"Now that you mention it –"

"Besides, I got my iPhone. I'll call if we get into any trouble. But this is just an outing like when I was in Girl Scouts. You're always saying I should get more exercise."

"You spend a lot of time sewing patchwork quilts with my friend Beau's wife. That's good for you and all – but a little fresh air can't hurt. Have a nice time, child."

Chapter Thirty-Two

Dog Days

Chief Jim Purdue's German Shepherd could have passed for a Timber Wolf, a big fellow with a gray pelt, yellow eyes, and fearsome fangs that made you want to say, "Oh what big teeth you have, Grandma!"

His weight was closer to 100 pounds than 80.

Nevertheless, Mörder had been trained to be a sniffer rather than a fighter. Not that he couldn't take down a perp if called upon. Weapons triggered his protective reflexes.

Police dog units are often referred to as K-9, a play on the word *canine*. They are trained to assist in searching for drugs and explosives, locating missing people, finding crime scene evidence, and attacking people targeted by the police.

Dogs have an extraordinary sense of smell. They possess up to 300 million olfactory receptors in their noses, compared to only six million in humans. And the part of a dog's brain that is devoted to analyzing smells is about 40 times greater than a person's. Tests have shown that some dogs can detect their owners or an object from a distance as great as 10 to 12 miles. Hard to believe.

Because of this sophisticated sense of smell, some K-9s specialize in detection – finding drugs or explosives or firearms. Dogs trained to detect cancer have an accuracy rate between 88% and 97%. Seizure Alert Dogs can warn a person of an oncoming epilepsy attack anywhere from 15 minutes to 12 hours before. Some dogs are trained to tell when cows are in heat by sniffing urine. Others can locate hard drives and other digital devices, very helpful when tracking down child pornographers.

In a forensic setting, cadaver dogs are trained to detect and locate concealed human remains or fluids such as blood.

A National Library of Medicine study showed that well trained dogs are "able to detect human cadaveric blood samples even when very low concentrations of blood were stored in the tubes ..."

As it turned out, **Mörder** had been a cadaver dog with the Chicago Police Department during his active years. Retired K-9 dogs often stay with their police handlers, but **Mörder** 's owner had died of a stroke, so he had been rehomed. Another cop – like Chief Jim Purdue – got precedence in the adoption process.

Mörder's training as a crime-scene dog earned him that intimidating name. By nature he was a sweetie ... but one with teeth.

~ ~ ~

Bootsie Purdue had adopted six dogs from the Strays & Rescues shelter that she ran. Although it was a no-kill animal shelter, the soft-hearted woman could not bear to see pups locked up in cages.

Mörder was her husband's push-back. If she was going to keep bringing pets home, so would he. He had adopted the retired K-9 through a policing website. Bootsie was steamed that he hadn't picked one of the needy dogs at her shelter.

"Police dogs need homes too," he'd replied. "They are especially deserving having served their communities so well. It's a dangerous job for dog and man alike."

He was getting no sympathy from his wife. She knew he mostly handed out parking tickets. The crime rate in Caruthers Corners was very low ... and the Quilters Club solved most of those cases to her husband's great chagrin.

Well, up until now.

Mörder was well trained, responded mostly to hand signals. Unfortunately, Jim didn't know any of them, so the big dog did mostly as he pleased. It didn't take him long to become a part of Bootsie's indolent pack of rescues.

While a humongous German Shepherd wouldn't have been her first choice, Bootsie believed in giving animals a Forever Home, so Mörder was quickly accepted and became more her dog than Jim's. Not being much of a dog person himself, he barely noticed this shift of loyalties.

The biggest aggravation was that Mörder now considered himself a lapdog, all 97 pounds crawling onto her generous lap. Not a very comfortable happening. But she was a true "Dog Mom."

When N'yen Madison asked if he could take the dog on an overnight camping trip, it was actually Bootsie who'd said yes, thinking an outing would be good for the big beast. Being cooped up in a small house with six other dogs could be confining. A camping trip with N'yen and his young friends might be good for the dog, she reasoned.

Go, boy, go!

Chapter Thirty-Three

Cabin Fever

Tilly had paid for the cabin in advance, so there was no problem checking in. Normally sleeping eight, No. 3 had plenty of room for Tilly, the three youngsters, and an oversized "wolf."

The plan was to wait till the first tour went into the cave the next morning, then sneak in behind them, keeping back so their presence would not be detected. Then at Blowing Bat Crawl, they would slide down to the third level to let Mörder sniff for any trace of blood on rocks that could have been used as a murder weapon.

The trick would be to do it without getting caught. It would be embarrassing for the wife and daughter of the Caruthers Corners mayor to get arrested for trespassing.

As their "insider," Aggie would pay to join that first tour, then hang back to make sure the cave entrance remained open for them. Nevertheless, she would leave the full price for the other three tickets in the tip jar as a show of honesty.

~ ~ ~

The morning's guide was Lester again. But he'd never laid eyes on Aggie Tidemore, so there was nothing to raise his suspicions. He took everyone through his spiel about caving safety and issued the hard hats and headlamps.

N'yen had borrowed hardhats and LED lights from his Uncle Freddie, who was Fire Chief in Caruthers Corners. The paramedic unit had an ample supply. His and Sissy's were a little large, but Tilly's fit perfectly.

The parking lot at Marengo Cave was nearly full that morning. Aside from people waiting for tours, there were lines for the popular Sky Climber attraction, the gemstone mining, Pedal Karting, a labyrinth called the Miner's Maze, and the large Gift Shop with its selection of shiny rocks, stuffed animals, and other themed souvenirs.

Sissy pointed out a park ranger truck in the lot. "Do you think that belongs to Hugo Marston?" she asked N'yen.

"Not likely. There are 240 park rangers in Southern Indiana. Probably one of them."

"Even so, keep your eyes open for that Marston guy," said Aggie. "I've never seen him, but you have."

"What would he be doing here?" wondered Sissy. "I doubt he'd have the nerve to show his face after just being arrested."

"Yeah, but he got released," said N'yen. "That alibi from his associate at National Institutes of Health did trick. His rep restored."

"That's why we're back here looking for new clues," Aggie nodded. "To save my Mom from any suspicion."

"Why would anyone suspect me?" said Tilly. "I didn't even know the dead man."

Aggie was pleased that her mother didn't bring up the subject of Morlocks or her former friend Herbie.

~ ~ ~

While Agnes Tidemore picked up her ticket for the first Crystal Palace tour of the day, her mother pretended to browse in the rock section at the back of the Gift Shop. But Tilly was only feigning interest in the shiny stones. After the hypnotic session with the Great Wizardini, she seemed to be totally over Crystal Power and rock therapy. And Morlocks.

N'yen and Sissy kept out of sight, mingling among the people watching the Pedal Kart races at the Springtime Speedway Racetrack. Kids competed with each other, knees pumping as they pedaled four-wheel vehicles around a curving gravel track. It looked like fun.

Lester the Guide assembled his tour group behind the Gift Shop, pattering on about caving safety and rules and proper behavior and such. "Line up behind me," he instructed. "Stay together. You won't get lost if you stay on the path. It's well lighted."

Aggie inched toward the back of the line. Out of the corner of her eye, she could see N'yen and Sissy heading this way, taking their time, as if casually strolling the grounds. Aggie's Mom was stepping off the Gift Shop's porch, preparing to meet them near the cave entrance.

"Okay, duck your heads," instructed Lester. "We will be descending to the second level. You will see Mirror Lake below us."

The group disappeared into the cave entrance, Aggie bringing up the rear. Tilly and Sissy and were waiting just outside, giving the tour a chance to move well ahead of them.

Meanwhile, N'yen had raced back to the cabin to retrieve Mörder. The big dog came loping out, pink tongue hanging in front of him like a necktie. His brown eyes were bright, reflecting the excitement of working again. A retractable leash was fastened to his harness.

"Hurry," hissed Aggie, waving at her companions from the door.

Tilly and the two youngsters squeezed through entrance, pulled by Mörder like an overzealous sled dog. Aggie caught the dog by his halter, holding him back. He started to whine with eagerness, but she fed him two dog biscuits that she had brought along from Tige's stash. That quieted him for the moment. Fortunately, she had a pocketful.

"Move slowly," advised N'yen *sotto voce*. "Use the handrail as you go down the steps. And watch your feet. The rocks can be slippery. Don't want this wolfhound pulling one of us off balance."

"Right," agreed Aggie. She fed the dog another biscuit.

"I wore knee pads under my jeans," said Sissy. "I banged myself up last trip. This limestone's hard when you fall on it."

"*Shhhh*," said Tilly. "The Morlock's might hear you."

That was the first sign of anything going wrong.

Chapter Thirty-Four

Crawling the Crawl

They could hear the tour group up ahead, chittering and chatting, admiring the underground formations. Lester's voice boomed as he pointed out sights like the Tobacco Shed, the Rocky Mountains, and massive flowstone deposits.

The sound of trickling and rushing water seemed to surround them. It had rained yesterday and the cave was very wet. Puddles from water seeping through surface cracks would create breeding sites for salamanders. The species found here would eventually leave the cave for a life above ground, returning to the same cave later to lay its eggs.

"Other animals such as isopods, millipedes, springtails, amphipods, and blind crayfish complete their entire life cycle inside the cave," whispered N'yen. "And over 100,000 endangered Indiana Bats make their home here." He'd done his research, a trait of the young Braniac.

Even Aggie was impressed.

~ ~ ~

The foursome proceeded cautiously, turning off their flashlights and headlamps, relying on the cave's lighting.

Making sure the tour was far ahead, they eased their way around the lake, **Mörder** leading the way.

Aggie could feel a breeze. "Where's that coming from?" she murmured.

"That's coming from a side passage," replied N'yen. "It's where we're going."

Just around a corner, passing through the floor-to-ceiling columns in Pillared Palace, they found the source of the wind gust – Blowing Bat Crawl.

"There it is," Sissy pointed to a dark crack behind a bronze plaque affixed to an upright stone. She kept her voice low so the tour wouldn't hear them.

Aggie continued to slip dog biscuits to Mörder. He remained quiet, having figured out the tradeoff. The canine certainly knew the answer to "Who's a good boy?"

N'yen went first, familiar with the crawlspace from his previous visit. Sissy followed him. Aggie and the German Shepherd came next, moving slowly to give him opportunity to sniff at the rocks. Tilly was reluctant to enter the hole, as if she feared meeting up with the killer. She was back to thinking it was a Morlock.

"Mom, come on," beckoned Aggie. Not that her mother could see her hand signals in the dark. The dog seemed fascinated with the crawlspace's low ceiling. Everything seemed claustrophobic to the teenager. She'd never liked tight spaces.

"Follow my light," coaxed the Vietnamese boy. "With yesterday's rain, this place is gonna be wet and muddy."

"Are there snakes down here?" squeaked Aggie as she touched something squishy.

"No snakes in the cave," N'yen assured her. "However, there are a few spiders, flies, fungus gnats, and cave beetles."

"Oweee."

"Aggie dear," said her mother. "that big dog you're handling won't let me pass. He keeps coming back this way, his nose to the ceiling."

"Probably smells bats," said Sissy. "Place is full of 'em."

"I haven't seen any bats," said Aggie.

"They roost farther back in the cave," answered N'yen. "We won't be going that far. If there's a rock used to kill Dr. Segal, it will be closer to the entrance of Blowing Bat Crawl where he was killed. We'll go to the bottom and work our way back up with the dog."

"That crazy hound's not going to the bottom," complained Tilly. "He refuses to go anywhere. He's sniffing and snorting like a Minotaur."

"Mom, Minotaurs lived in caves in Crete, not here in Southern Indiana."

"Dear, I'm not saying Minotaurs are real. I know they are mythological creatures. I was merely using them as a simile. They teach you about similes at Yale, don't they?'"

"Oh, sorry."

"This dog is having a conniption back here," Tilly continued without giving Minotaurs another thought. "Maybe he's onto something."

"Okay, back up everybody," commanded N'yen. "Let's see what Mörder has turned up." He scrambled around, reversing his course.

Tilly climbed back out of Blowing Bat Crawl. Aggie had trouble getting past the German Shepherd, who refused to relinquish his position. Sissy scooted past, leaving her boyfriend on the downward side of the dog.

Judging by the K-9's reaction, you'd think he'd come up with something. He was snuffling like a hog who'd located truffles. "Easy boy, let me check this out," muttered N'yen.

The boy extracted a brown bottle and some cotton swabs from his belt pack. "Hold on a minute while I test the ceiling where Mörder is sniffing," he told them.

"What's that?" asked Aggie. "I thought you said you didn't have any luminol."

"I don't. So I'm pulling a MacGyver, making do with hydrogen peroxide."

"Hydrogen peroxide – like I have in my medicine cabinet?"

"Right," confirmed her cousin. "If hemoglobin is present, the hydrogen peroxide decomposes to yield oxygen that in turn oxidizes the phenolphtalin to phenolphthalein. Since the solution is basic, a pink color develops indicating the presence of blood. The test is very sensitive, but it cannot distinguish human blood from animal blood."

"If there's any blood down here, it's likely human," surmised Aggie. "No animals are allowed in here, except maybe a Pekinese in its owner's arms."

"Not even a Pekinese gets down Blowing Bat Crawl," said N'yen. "Pets are only allowed on the walking tour along the lighted pathway."

"Okay, Mr. Genius, what does it show?"

"It –"

~ ~ ~

"Never mind what it shows," came a gruff voice from outside the hole. "Come on out before you get hurt."

"Who's that?" asked N'yen.

"Some guy with a gun," reported Aggie, now outside on the paved path winding through Pillared Palace.

"It's that Morlock," said Tilly. "I can tell by those two glowing eyes."

"Glowing eyes? Those are my headlamps, lady."

"You killed that professor," she accused.

"You're crazy. I was cleared of that. Benjy Bartle gave me an alibi."

"That's because he was in on the murder with you," Sissy spoke up. "The two of you kilt him together." Blurting out her theory just as quickly as it formed in her mind.

"That's a lie –!" He swung the pistol in her direction.

At that precise moment, 97 pounds of unbridled fury hit the man like a speeding Mack truck. The K-9 dog had been trained to react to drawn guns. The three-inch teeth locked around Hugo Marston's wrist like a clamp, bringing blood and a lot of pain. His Sig Sauer .45 when flying into the darkness.

"Agggggh," screamed the downed park ranger. "Get that monster off me!"

"Don't move," Aggie warned the man as she pulled Mörder off using his leash like a tug-of-war. "One twitch and I'll sic him on you again."

"I recognize you," said Tilly. "It wasn't a Morlock who killed that professor. It was you I saw standing next to his body."

"Yeah, yeah. It was me you saw. But I didn't kill him. He banged his head on that overhead ledge as he was coming out of the crawl. He hit it pretty hard, but I couldn't believe it killed him. When you saw me and screamed, I panicked and scrambled down the hole. Didn't come out till after the police finished poking about. I hid up above the waterfall. They didn't come that far."

"How come that NIH doctor gave you an alibi?" asked Sissy. "Said you left together."

"He's my brother-in-law – my wife's older brother. Bartle was her maiden name. He knew I'd never kill anybody, even if the guy was having an affair with Trudy."

"But the baby your wife just had, Dr. Segal was the father," said Sissy. "That gives you motive."

"No, he wasn't. I had it checked. A DNA test showed that Hugo Jr. is mine. The baby's the reason I decided to forgive my wife and keep the marriage together. Yeah, I hated Jonathan Segal, but I didn't kill him."

"Sure you did," said Aggie, feeling safe with the snarling German Shepherd at her side. The dog was obviously well-trained. But if he decided to attack the man again, she couldn't have held him back.

"No, he didn't," said N'yen from inside the crawlspace. He poked his head out like a groundhog looking for his shadow.

"What do you mean he didn't?" retorted Sissy. "What's he doing here with a gun, if he ain't guilty as Sin?"

"Dunno what he's doing here, but the evidence says Dr. Segal cracked his head on the limestone rock as he was climbing out of Blowing Bat Crawl. My swab turned pink, showing there was blood right where Mörder's carrying-on said it was."

"See?" said the park ranger. "Just like I told you."

"Then what are you doing here if you ain't guilty," accused Sissy.

"I came back to retrieve Jonathan Segal's helmet from where I hid it in the piles of breakdown beyond the waterfall."

Aggie said, "Why would you do that?"

"Segal had taken off his hard hat too soon, hit his head on the low limestone rock. I guess he dropped the hardhat when he hit his head and it tumbled into the crawl. As I made my escape, I must have unthinkingly scooped it up. Didn't even realize I had it till I hunkered down to hide. By then, my fingerprints were all over it. That's what I was looking for last week when they caught me, not the rock hammer. I was afraid if anyone found that helmet with my fingerprints on it, it might be said I pulled it off his head and hit him."

"How do we know that's not what happened?" said Tilly. "I saw you standing over his body."

"You heard the boy. He found blood on that rock overhang. Proves Jonathan Segal hit his head there rather than me braining him with a hammer or whatever."

"Then why'd you pull a gun on us?" said Sissy. Still not convinced.

"I slipped into the cave when nobody was looking. I didn't expect to find you busybodies here. It startled me."

"Hey, said Aggie, "we're not busybodies. We're the Quilters Club."

Epilogue

A grand jury ruled Dr. Jonathan Livingston Segal's death to be accidental. For the second time, charges against Hugo Marston were dropped. He and his family moved to North Dakota for a ranger's job at the Fort Abraham Lincoln State Park, home of the On-A-Slant Indian Village. There are very few caves in that state. That was a plus.

Benjamin Bartle got off with a strong warning about giving false testimony to law enforcement officers. The NIH suspended him for two months without pay.

No charges would be filed against Tilly Tidemore either. But Tilly and the three youngsters got a stern lecture from Sheriff Jake Barneswell about trespassing in Marengo Cave. Fortunately, the fact they had left money equivalent to the price of admission in the Gift Shop tip jar was taken into account.

Aggie flew back to New Haven to continue her pre-law studies at Yale. N'yen returned to his astrophysics classes at Northwestern. Both were making the Dean's List.

Sissy won a prize at the annual Watermelon Festival for her Shooting Star Quilt. She received particular praise for her masterful use of the backstitch. Lizzie was so proud of her. The Quilters Club took her to Cozy Café for a watermelon milkshake to celebrate.

Later that month Sissy's performance in *West Side Story* got rave reviews. Her picture appeared in the *Burpyville*

Gazette along with the caption: **A Star Is Born.** N'yen sent flowers.

That same month Hoople Mansion was deeded over to the town to become the new Hoople Senior Living Center. Mayor Mark Tidemore joined Maddy for the ribbon-cutting. Governor Eric Holcomb made a speech. As the facility's new director, Marybelle Olsen accepted a symbolic key. Ernst Hegler and his sister Mary Alice were among the new residents.

Maddy and Beau built another Victorian-style house on Melon Pickers Row. She paid especial attention to the kitchen, eager to get back to baking her famous watermelon upside down cakes. She loved her new home.

Maddy also bought new houses for Tilly and Freddie in the up-and-coming Melon Hill section of Caruthers Corners; then she paid off the mortgage on Bill's condo in Chicago.

Tilly was – more or less – over her schizoid view of the world. No more unicorns or dragons. It wasn't clear whether she still believed in Morlocks, but she didn't talk about them. Apparently, Herbie had returned to Suicide Cave down in Salem, Indiana. Tilly was now interested in psychotherapy. Sigmund Freud was her new hero.

Having accused the wrong man in the Dr. Jonathan Livingston Segal death, Maddy and her friends agreed that the Quilters Club should forego investigating murders and stick to its sewing. A sad outcome, but Police Chief Jim Purdue gave a sigh of relief. He had never approved of their interference with official police business.

Mark Tidemore was elected to another term as mayor. Life in Caruthers Corners seemed to be back to normal ... almost.

That was before the great Shakespearean actor Adolphus Everly Anderson came to town with his Merry Times acting troupe. His rendition of Puck in *A Midsummer's Night's Dream* would be his last performance. Some said he died of a heart attack in Act 3 Scene 2.

The Quilters Club suspected it was murder. But would they dare investigate? You will find the answer in the next book, *Quilting on a Midsummer's Night.*

Author's Note

Although the descriptions of Marengo Cave are mostly accurate, the cave and its staff are used fictitiously. Blowing Bat Crawl is a real side passage in the cave. Marengo Cave is a wonderful natural phenomenon in Southern Indiana that is well worth a visit.

Marengo is a delightful small town in Crawford County, Indiana. However, its citizens and environs are the product of the author's imagination.

Caruthers Corners is inspired by several towns in northeastern Indiana – but it remains real in Marjory Sorrell Rockwell's mind. Yours too, we hope.

Mental illnesses – particularly schizophreniform disorders – are serious conditions and their depiction in this book is meant to call attention to it as a problem that deserves more study. Better treatments are needed for these debilitating psychological disorders.

Thank you for reading.
Please review this book. Reviews
help others find Absolutely Amazing eBooks and
inspire us to keep providing these marvelous tales.
If you would like to be put on our email list
to receive updates on new releases,
contests, and promotions, please go to
AbsolutelyAmazingEbooks.com and sign up.

About the Author

Marjory Sorrell Rockwell says needlecraft arts – quilting, crocheting, knitting – are pastimes every woman can appreciate. And she particularly loves quiltmaking. "It's like painting with cloth," she says. But when not quilting she writes mysteries about a Midwestern sleuth not unlike herself, a middle-aged lady with an unpredictable family and loyal friends. And she's a big fan of watermelon pie.

Quilter Club Mysteries

Visit Maddy's new website...

quiltersclubmysteries.com/

Take a tour of Caruthers Corners and the surrounding countryside. Meet Maddy's family and friends. Get a complete list of all the characters who have appeared in the entire Quilter's Club Mysteries book series.

What's more, you'll learn lots about quilting. There's a free quilt pattern. A dictionary of quilting terms. Even a Quilt Gallery showing some of Maddy's favorite quilt patterns.

No fees, no charges. Just fun.

For sales, editorial information, subsidiary rights information or a catalog, please write or phone or e-mail
AbsolutelyAmazingEbooks
Manhanset House
Shelter Island Hts., New York 11965-0342, US
Tel: 212-427-7139
www.AbsolutelyAmazingEbooks.com
bricktower@aol.com
www.IngramContent.com

For sales in the UK and Europe please contact our distributor,
Gazelle Book Services
White Cross Mills
Lancaster, LA1 4XS, UK
Tel: (01524) 68765 Fax: (01524) 63232
email: jacky@gazellebooks.co.uk

www.ingramcontent.com/pod-product-compliance
Lightning Source LLC
Chambersburg PA
CBHW070523260626
47161CB00004B/1621